LUCY LEHMAN

THE ADVENTURES OF GERALD THE GENIE
A novel for middle-grade readers

Dedicated to Sarah, Mira and Leah Lehman,
my inspiration and first readers

With gratitude to Nora Cohen for editing the manuscript

CHAPTER ONE

Geniometry

S EVERAL YEARS AGO I was hiking in the southwest of the United States. After several hours, I stopped to rest in the shade of a large oak tree and spotted a knot in its trunk. Brushing aside some leaves, I discovered a leather journal hidden underneath. Neatly written in block letters, it was an account of a genie's adventures traveling around the globe to grant wishes to people he met. As the sun rose high in the sky, I sat and read the whole story, fascinated by what he'd described.

Then I met the genie, Gerald, himself. He'd been hiding nearby in the grass next to a cracked and dirty bottle. He'd spotted me with his journal and came to see who'd taken the book from his hiding place. He was very worried that I might keep it, but when I assured him that I wouldn't, he became friendly.

We sat for hours while he told me more about his adventures, starting with the College of Geniometry where he'd learned how to make magic. Although the college had existed for a long time, very few people know about it, since genies are a secret society. To become a genie was considered a great honor. Professors who'd practiced Geniometry centuries before trained an elite class of elves once a year.

Gerald pointed to the barn nearby that looked as if it might collapse in a gust of wind. The College of Geniometry had set up shop in its ruins, after people abandoned it when the roof caught fire. He took me inside, describing how all the genies had loved its musty rafters, even though the roof leaked when it rained. The hayloft, scarred by flames, had served as his classroom. An old cart missing a wheel, and once used for hauling hay, was the only thing that remained on the dusty floor. Propped up on a cement block, it had somehow escaped the flames that had scorched the barn's walls. Gerald described how the professors had used the cart as a table for food, when they gave large parties for all the animals living nearby.

He told me he'd always wanted to become a genie but never dreamed he'd be chosen. All he'd ever known was the farmland on the prairie filled with peaceful fields and friendly animals. The college accepted no more than twelve elves a year, and only those who were friendly, kind, and willing to learn new things. He understood that if he was admitted there would be a lot to learn, but he wasn't afraid of hard work. Gerald applied and waited anxiously to see if he'd be chosen. Other elves who'd been mischievous or unkind were turned away.

The year before, his friend Alfie hadn't been admitted because he'd played a nasty trick on a farmer. He'd locked all the doors to his house for an entire day, and the farmer and his family had to climb out in and out of the windows. Suzette was turned down because she was too mischievous and teased the horses in the fields by blowing dandelions fuzz in their eyes. They bolted away in fright, afraid to graze in the corral for days after.

Gerald was known to be playful, good natured and kind. His favorite sport was riding on the backs of the frogs in a nearby pond, where they leaped over the lily pads in the shadow of a large oak tree. He pretended to be a jockey on a racecourse and organized games where the fastest frog got a prize of ten dead flies. The frogs loved the game and waited for Gerald every day.

Besides the frogs, the birds on the farm were his closest friends. He helped robins build their nests in the trees behind the barn and protected the birds from the magpies that tried to steal their eggs. All the animals in the fields liked him as well. He was friendly and never teased them or played tricks. They all voted for Gerald with enthusiasm.

The professors at the college had held a big party in the barn to announce the new class. Invited were all the candidates, plus the birds, frogs, horses, dogs, and cats that lived nearby and who'd elected the class. The professors offered them a generous picnic and served it on the old hay wagon. The animals feasted on worms, bugs, hay, meat bones and fish. Elves don't eat since they are sprites who exist on sunlight and fresh air, but they enjoyed watching their friends consume the spread. After the meal, the professors announced who'd been accepted. Gerald was overjoyed when he found out that he'd be in the class.

He described at length all the courses the college taught. First he had to learn how to read, write, and solve math problems. Those classes were taught by Professor Arthur Aardvark and took a lot of memorizing. Gerald was a fast learner, and in a week, he could count to a million in five minutes. Then Professor Morton Mongoose taught the elves geography. They memorized the customs of each nation and learned common phrases of all the languages spoken around the globe. If a genie found himself in Egypt, he needed to speak basic Arabic; when in Rome Italian; or for Japan, Japanese. Learning all those languages took another three weeks, but Gerald had an excellent memory. His teachers praised him, and Gerald's head expanded like a balloon inflating, after learning all that information.

There only remained one class to master. Called *Magic and Wisdom*, it was taught by the headmaster, Professor William Wombatt. He'd taught the class to genies throughout the world, and it was famously difficult. Each student had to meet with him individually to learn how to use good judgment and common sense. He told all his students that these were the most important skills all genies would need.

Professor Wombatt was sitting on his bottle when Gerald arrived. The professor, who'd been an elf hundreds of years before he'd become a genie, had yellowing, wrinkled skin and eyes that shone like black marbles.

He began by saying, "First I need you to understand what we genies can do, and what we can't accomplish. We can't cure the sick or bring the dead back to life. We never grant wishes based on revenge or anger. That poisons everything. We have an honor code. We cannot take revenge or act cruelly on behalf of our clients. We can give people money, but it's usually better to give them the things they need rather than let them spend the funds themselves, because they often handle money unwisely. Beware of people who wish to become rich. Too much wealth can produce misery. We'll discuss all this later in detail. But first, Gerald, I am going to give you a test of judgment. Before you answer my question, remember: you can only grant three wishes to any one client, and twenty total. You have to guard those precious wishes and not waste even one. Here is the question: imagine that you land in Venice, Italy and meet a woman who wishes her entire house to be painted purple, inside and out. What would you do?”

“That's easy!” Gerald replied. “I would speak to the *Signora* in Italian and use the proper magic spell to paint her house purple, as she wishes. “

“But Gerald, how would you phrase that wish? You must be very exact.”

“I would say, ‘*I'll now make all the house purple*’ and utter the correct incantation.”

“Would you paint the floors, the walls and the ceilings all the same color?”

“Of course. That's what the client wants, right? “

“Are you sure? Consider the problem, Gerald. Would you want to live in a house where every surface was purple? Imagine how it would appear.”

Gerald gazed around the old barn. It's brown walls were now faded to a dusty tan. Stalks of golden hay and corncobs dotted the dirt floor, while beams of milky sunlight streaming through the cracked windows. The wagon had once been red, but the paint had chipped off and the wooden frame was now gray. The muted colors made the barn cozy and calming. He realized that if everything were purple, it would be very dark and scary. “I think I understand,” he told the professor. “No one would want to live in a house painted a dark color. What if I agreed to paint the walls purple, and left the floor and ceiling white? That would be better, right?”

“If you had granted the woman's wish for an all purple house without thinking about it first, the result probably wouldn't have made her happy for very long. Then to change that, you would need to use the second of her three wishes.”

"I see. I would have wasted a wish."

"There are many shades of purple. Some shades are almost black. The dark walls would make any room appear smaller. Think, Gerald! What should you have done first, before granting the woman her wish for a purple house?"

"Perhaps I should have asked her if she wanted all the walls, plus the floor and ceiling purple."

"What else?"

Gerald took a moment to think, but he was so confused he didn't know what to reply. "Tell me what I should have done, Professor, please."

"Should you have asked your client what shade of purple she wanted? Gerald, the lesson today is about making sure clients get what they want – not what they they think they want. Remember, three wishes are not many. If you weren't careful, you would have needed to use up all three wishes to make that woman happy and fix the mess you'd created. First, you would have painted the whole house –inside and outside, from top to bottom – a brilliant purple. Then the second wish, when she was unhappy with what'd you'd created, would have been to repaint the floor and ceilings another color, and the third would have been to change the dark purple to a gentle shade, perhaps the delicate violet of iris petals. And then, a week later when the client would have been sick and tired of seeing her house all one color, you could no longer help her. You would have wasted her three wishes. So, Gerald, please explain the lesson you just learned."

"Never paint a whole house purple?"

Professor Wombatt laughed. "No, Gerald. The lesson is: "*Be wise in the wishes you grant.* Make sure you give clients something they truly need or want. Maybe you should have painted only one wall purple at first, to see if the *Signora* liked the shade. That might have been one thing to try. There were other solutions, if you think about it. You should have talked to her and found a way to make her happy, but you needed to be cautious and practical.

"Here's an example of a mistake a former genie named Esmeralda made. She landed in Ecuador where she met a woman named Rosalba with ten children. Senora Rosalba was exhausted trying to keep those children clean. She spent hours scrubbing their clothing in soapy water until her fingers were red and chapped. Afterwards she had to pin all those heavy, wet garments on a clothesline. Rosalba begged the genie to help her. Esmeralda proudly conjured up a washing machine and dryer, but her two wishes were wasted. Can you figure out why?"

"No, I don't understand why that was a mistake. It sounds like a great solution to me."

"Esmeralda didn't use her eyes to guide her. She didn't notice that Rosalba's house had no electricity or running water. The woman lit her house by lanterns and cooked over an open fire. All their water came from a well, not a faucet. Suppose you, Gerald, had been there in Ecuador and met Rosalba, but you were wise enough to see the problems before you granted a wish. How do you think you could have helped this poor mother?"

Gerald was stumped. "I don't know, Professor Wombatt. Could I, as a genie, have installed power lines?"

The professor said. "Not possible. We don't have any magic for that. We can't produce a power grid, nor can we supply coal, natural gas or any polluting sources of energy for our clients. Most common wishes we grant are for rain, machines, food, or animals. Other magic spells are far more advanced and must be used with great care. To help Rosalba, the genie could have given her money to hire someone to help with the laundry. The salary for an assistant would have been good for the village as well. Everyone there was very poor and there were few jobs to earn money.

"You see," the professor added, "solutions are not always simple, and granting wishes takes some thought."

Gerald nodded. "I would have had to think very hard to find that answer."

"Being a genie is more challenging than it would first appear. Come back tomorrow and we'll practice the importance of using your powers of judgment before granting wishes."

Gerald continued to see Wombatt for two weeks, and each day he found the professor's questions more and more challenging. Each example he gave took a lot of thought before proposing a good solution.

After two weeks, the professor gave Gerald a final question to see if he was ready to become a genie. He was very nervous, but Professor Wombatt said, "Don't worry. You'll do fine if you remember to reason carefully and not propose a simple solution. I'm going to pretend to be a client with a wish, and you can ask me questions to help decide how to grant it. After that I'll tell you how wise your solution was."

The exam problem concerned a twelve year old boy named Ernesto Negron from Spain who wanted a sailboat. Gerald soon found out that Ernesto didn't even know how to swim, much less sail a boat. Whenever he proposed a solution Wombatt challenged it, until Gerald figured out how to keep Ernesto safe before he tried sailing. They discussed the problem all afternoon until the professor said, "We'll end the exam here. Although you did well, you can see that sometimes there are wishes we can't easily grant, and problems we can't solve. As much as you want to help, you may not be able to grant a wish even though you tried your best. Sometimes we genies have to disappoint. Congratulations on passing the course on wisdom for genies! Today you did well. You're now ready to learn our secret spells."

Professor Aardvark taught the secret incantations that they would need. There were many, and they were hard to learn but exciting when they worked. Gerald first mastered the formula for producing animals. Then he memorized the one for changing someone's hair to another color and making things larger or smaller, and another for giving clients small possessions they wanted. Those were the easiest. The incantations for making things appear or disappear were harder and took a lot of practice. There were many more to memorize.

When the students pronounced the magic spells correctly, a puff of green smoke and a clap of thunder would follow. As the twelve learned them, the clearing surrounding the barn was filled with green smoke, and small claps of thunder echoed through the treetops.

Gerald changed his friend Marie's hair from blond to blue, and Marie changed Gerald's shape from small and round to skinny as a toothpick. Then they changed each other back into how they'd been before. The students knew that many clients would ask them to produce rain. They practiced milking so much rain from the clouds that the prairie bloomed with bright wildflowers among the stalks of corn. However when Professor Wombatt saw that, he warned them never to make it rain if the soil was dry. He said that on parched earth too much rain might be dangerous and create a flood. At last the class had memorized all the incantations and were ready to graduate.

At the graduation ceremony Professor Aardvark gave a

speech reminding them of their goals. He reminded them that after they granted twenty wishes, they would lose the ability to make magic.

At last Professor Aardvark handed out the diplomas. Gerald's read:

The College of Geniometry attests to the fact that Elf Gerald has fulfilled all the requirements for becoming a genie. He has sworn to follow all the cardinal rules below. This diploma enables him to use his magic powers to grant twenty wishes to his clients, according to the rules below:

Each genie may grant twenty wishes, no more than three per person.

A genie must always obey the Geniometry honor code and choose wisely in fulfilling those wishes.

He or she must always remember to use kindness balanced by common sense.

After the speech, the graduates received a small beret, and a pouch to hold their genie phones and the diploma. They had to carry that precious document at all times as a reminder of the powers it bestowed. Gerald thought that he'd never felt prouder in his life.

Finally, Professor Wombatt recited a master incantation that turned them from elves to genies. The spell was so complicated that it took him five minutes to recite. There followed a huge flash of green smoke and a deafening chorus of thunderclaps, like exploding fireworks. All the genies cheered with excitement while the three professors applauded. The ceremony ended with a joyful musical chorus performed by the birds and frogs.

It was time for the genies to choose a bottle in which to travel the globe. Outside the barn stood an assortment in many beautiful colors. There were large ones with wide necks; tall, narrow ones erect like soldiers; and some round jugs like toadstools. Gerald spotted a delicate blue one with a narrow neck. He raced across the field to claim it. As he gazed out through the glass, the prairie appeared tinted blue-green like ocean water. Gerald was delighted with his new home.

Finally Professor Wombatt called forth a Mighty Wind to lift all the bottles one by one and bear the genies around the globe. Snug in his blue bottle, Gerald sailed smoothly over the clouds. He was off on his first adventure! He couldn't wait to meet his first client.

CHAPTER TWO

Nigel Consobolo

GERALD'S FIRST CLIENT was a young boy in Chile who wanted a bicycle, which took a single wish. It was an easy bit of magic with no challenges to face, and he relaxed as he sailed away with the Magic Wind.

Next, he met a couple in Madrid who wanted to have babies after being childless for years. Gerald was delighted to help and gave them triplets with three wishes, and when he left they were very busy caring for the infants. He realized that giving them just one child might have been more practical and wiser, and felt guilty that he hadn't thought about the problem carefully. He remembered Professor Wombat's warnings and vowed to do better.

When the Mighty Wind came for him after Spain, it carried the blue bottle across several continents to Kenya in northeast Africa. Gerald landed at a village with straw huts clinging to bamboo poles. All the plants in the gardens surrounding the huts were wilting or had died in the intense heat. The bottle lay on the dusty soil until a boy searching among the plants picked it up. Gerald popped out and introduced himself. "What's your name, and how old are you?" he asked.

"My name is Nigel Consobolo, and I'm sixteen," the boy replied. "I'm delighted to make your acquaintance, Gerald." He tried to shake Gerald's hand, but the genie's palm was so tiny he couldn't grasp it. "I'm searching in this vegetable patch for a squash or two to cook, but most of the vines have died in this heat wave. We've nothing left to eat."

Nigel spoke fluent English, and he told Gerald that he'd learned to read and write in a missionary school. When the genie offered him a wish, he knew exactly what he wanted. "I need to find food for us. Everyone here in the village is very hungry. It's been a particularly hot year, and all the wells are almost dry. We're forty people, and we can't grow crops without water. We'll starve to death before the rainy season. But if I had a helicopter, I could fly over to that far away mountain where wild goats, boars and fat birds are as thick as bees in honey. Juicy berries and other fruit grow on the bushes under the shade of those tall trees." He pointed to a large hill in the distance. "Then I could pick the fruit, hunt, and bring food home for everyone to eat, until it cools off and the rains come. Then we can plant more crops. But until that day we will remain hungry! Can you help me? Will you get me a helicopter?"

"I don't think your idea would work. It's true I could recite a spell and produce a helicopter, but who'll fly it? It takes a lot of practice to be a pilot. It also takes fuel, and I don't have any powers to provide diesel fuel for an engine, or gasoline for a car. There's no magic for petroleum products. How about a bicycle to search for plants around here?"

Nigel pointed to the heavy shrubs around his village. "I own a bicycle but can't ride it through the woods. There are no plants we can eat that grow nearby. I'm sure I'd know how to fly if you can get me a helicopter. I've read books about planes, and I've always wanted to be a pilot. In any case, if I don't try something, we may all starve."

Gerald saw how thin Nigel was, but he didn't know how he could help. He thought he'd have to refuse his wish and felt sad. Professor Wombatt had told him that sometimes it was wiser to say no to an impossible wish than to produce a disaster where no one would be happy.

Then he had an idea. "Perhaps I can get you a plane, a glider. It doesn't take fuel, and it can't be that hard to steer. What do you think?"

"I know a glider needs something to set it aloft. Usually a plane with an engine or a truck will pull the glider to help it gain altitude. How can you manage that, Gerald? We have no airfield here."

The genie was stumped until again he had an inspiration. "I believe I can summon enough thrust to get a glider into the sky with a little help from the College of Geniometry!" He could try sending a request on his genie phone to the professors for a one-time emergency assist from the Mighty Wind to come and propel the plane airborne. It might just work. There was one narrow dirt road leading out of the village that would be just wide enough for a glider's wheels. He explained his idea, and Nigel said, "It's worth a try."

"It's a big chance we'll be taking if you really want me to produce a glider. I'd have to come along with you in case we need two more wishes to get you food. Do you think you can fly a glider?"

"I want to try! I'll just go get my bow and arrow and tell my mum I'll be back as soon as possible with food." He ran off to his hut before Gerald could tell him he didn't like the idea of hunting animals, even to feed people who were desperately hungry. He decided to ask Nigel to leave the bow and arrow behind.

Professor Aardvark approved the emergency request for the Magic Wind. Gerald prayed that his plan would work. He pronounced an incantation for the glider, and when the villagers heard thunder and saw green smoke, they all looked up at the cloudless sky with amazement. The glider suddenly appeared on a nearby narrow dirt road, alarming the whole village. The chief told everyone that this must be dangerous magic and warned Nigel not to get in it, but the boy said that he had to risk trying.

The plane was old and small, just big enough for a pilot in the cockpit and a space for storage in back. Nigel climbed into the cockpit and carefully placed Gerald's bottle wrapped in straw at his feet for safety. "I think I understand the stick control and the foot pedals," he said. "I've been reading about airplanes ever since I was eight. We'll be fine. Don't worry!" His mother begged him not to go, but he said, "Mum, don't worry. I'm a man now and want to help the village. I trust in my new friend Gerald. We won't be long, I promise, and we'll bring back food for everyone."

All the people of the village gathered to watch the glider take off. Nigel waved goodbye, and the brave ones called out "Good luck. Have a safe trip!"

The Mighty Wind arrived on schedule in a huge spiral of dust, tugging the plane first forward and then upward. "We're airborne, Gerald," Nigel said. "I'm going to head for the mountain. Are you alright?"

Gerald was very hot in his straw wrap, but he sent a small puff of green smoke up to let Nigel know that he was fine. The glider wobbled slightly and then banked toward the mountain before leveling off. Nigel whooped with joy when he realized that he was piloting the aircraft successfully. When the plane was flying smoothly, Nigel unwrapped the genie, and he popped his torso out of the blue bottle to watch their flight.

All went well until the boy tried to land the plane on the mountain, but there was no flat land for the glider to set down. The little aircraft skimmed so low above the treetops that Gerald could hear the birds singing just below the wings.

"I'm afraid we're going to crash," Nigel said. "Hold on; I can't control the glider any longer." As they came down the far side of the mountain, an updraft from the cliff below lifted the aircraft once more aloft, and they soared above a grassy savannah, scaring a herd of zebras that ran away in panic. A little further on they saw a cheetah poised in the grass to chase some giraffes that were nibbling at leaves in the treetops. He spied a large herd of elephants swatting their tails at flies and slowly walking through the undergrowth. Gerald was thrilled with the trip. He'd had his doubts about whether the glider would work, and so far the flight was amazing.

The plane began to lose height several minutes later. "Hold on Gerald," said Nigel. "I don't think we're going to make it back to the mountain." The plane slowed down and dipped lower, and as the wheels touched the earth he fought to keep the glider from flipping over. It shook so badly Gerald thought it would shatter on impact and was afraid that the blue bottle would break during the bumpy landing. Yet somehow the glider remained intact and the blue bottle in one piece.

They found themselves on a dusty plain with a few weeds poking out between pebbles and clumps of earth. Cradling the bottle, Nigel climbed out of the cockpit. There was a small city on the horizon. He tucked the blue bottle into his waist and began to hike toward it. "Gerald, my mate," he said, "I don't know how we're ever going to get any food to bring home. I'm not sure that we'll even be able to get that old glider off the ground again. I think I saw a crack in one wing. I hope you have enough wishes left to save us." Gerald was hoping the same thing. The situation didn't appear promising.

The town, when they arrived, was nothing more than a market street surrounded by small mud shops. Nevertheless, people greeted them in a friendly manner and asked from where they'd come. "I've come by plane in search of food for my people. Our village is far away—on the other side of the mountain, and I need provisions for my family and the tribe," Nigel told them. "We have nothing to eat because of the drought."

An old man was listening sympathetically and said, "Just over there is the town grocer, Peter M'Boya. Why don't you ask him for some food?" He pointed to a shop where beans, squash, carrots, corn and cassava were displayed in large bins, and in a wire cage live chickens were clucking and fighting over grains of corn.

Peter M'Boya was a large man with his tummy hanging over a pair of ripped shorts. On his big chest he wore a stained T-shirt with the words *The Rolling Stones in Concert* written in cursive on a yellow background. Gerald wondered what the words meant: where were the stones going and how could they perform in a concert? He wanted to ask Nigel, but the boy was talking to Peter.

"Well, of course I can help you," said Peter, "if you can pay for the food. I have to eat too."

"I have no money," Nigel replied. "Please have pity on us. It's been a dry season, and all our crops have withered.

We're very hungry and will starve before the rains come and we can plant again."

"What can you barter, then?" the big man asked.

"Nothing. I can't give you our plane, because without it I can't get home."

"I'm terribly sorry, my lad, but…."

That's when Gerald popped out of the bottle. "Hello, Peter. My name is Gerald and I can pay you for the groceries. Tell me a fair price and I'll give you the money."

Peter jumped back in surprise and said to Nigel, "I didn't know that you travel with your own *spirit*. I see he has great powers. Please don't let him punish me! I meant you no harm." He fell to his knees in fear.

"Don't worry," said Gerald, "I don't hurt people. I come in peace. For the food we buy I can pay you in dollars. Just give me a fair price for groceries to feed a village of forty for a month."

A crafty smile crept over Peter's face. "A thousand dollars then for some fruit, two dozen chickens, some hens to lay eggs, and several crates of vegetables. Little "Spirit, I am of course giving *you* a special price since you have such powers!"

"No, that's not a fair price! Even a genie like myself knows that one thousand dollars is far too much." Gerald remembered Professor Wombatt's warning about giving people too much money, so he was determined not to pay Peter more than the worth of the food. "I'll give you two hundred," he said.

"Seven hundred."

"Four hundred."

"You are taking the food out of my own children's mouths at that price! It pains me to even think what a loss I will suffer for this." Peter wiped his eyes and sniffed as if the very thought was painful. "However, *for you*…four-fifty. That's my final price."

Before he could change his mind, Gerald said the incantation to produce four hundred fifty dollars, and the money fell from the sky in a large envelope that landed at Peter's feet. The butcher didn't even appear to notice the green smoke or hear the thunderclap overhead as, crowing with joy, he seized the envelope. "Thank you, little Spirit! I wish you a safe trip home."

"Wait," said Nigel. "We still have to get aloft. Peter, will you help us load up the glider and then lend us a truck and driver to pull our plane, so it can take off?"

"And what will I get for that?" Peter asked.

Nigel opened his mouth to reply but Gerald had an answer. "I will give you a brand-new motorcycle, the newest model, and you can give your children rides on it and show it to everyone here. That will make you the most important man in the village.

"Yes! Yes! I love that idea." Peter did a little dance with joy before getting a hungry gleam in his eyes. "In fact, I would like a Harley-Davidson Sportster Iron. I've seen photos of it in *Racing and Track Magazine*."

"The best one can buy, of course," Gerald replied, although honestly he had no idea about motorcycle brands. "I'll make it happen at dawn. Tomorrow you will find one outside your shop. All your friends will come and admire it." Gerald didn't bother to tell him that gasoline was not included in the deal. He was hoping that this bargain didn't violate the genie honor code and wouldn't be considered a bribe. When he saw how happy Peter was, he decided he'd chosen well.

"Splendid!" Peter said. "And so I will borrow my friend

Franklin's truck, and we will load up all the provisions and tow your plane." It was clear he thought he'd made a good bargain.

A few hours later, with the crates of groceries and cackling chickens crammed into the storage space behind the cockpit, the glider took off. This time Nigel knew how to approach the mountain and let the air currents send him high enough to steer the plane home. When they arrived, the whole village cheered and surrounded the plane. The chief carried Nigel on his shoulders and praised him as their savior.

That night there was a big celebration with a fire blazing and food cooked in big iron pots. Fragrant smoke rose high into the sky, while the villagers sang and danced. They proclaimed Nigel a hero, although he told everyone that it was really a spirit called Gerald who had saved the day. The people of the tribe thought Nigel was being too modest and doubted his story about a genie, because the blue bottle was not to be found. In the excitement Nigel had forgotten that he'd left it in the glider, where it lay hidden among the straw on the floor of the cockpit.

One month later the rainy season arrived and gently watered the dry earth, allowing the villagers to plant more crops. During one windy storm a wing fell off the glider, and the broken plane somersaulted like tumbleweed into the bushes. The bottle spilled onto the road, where at last the Mighty Wind found it and carried Gerald out over the vast Indian Ocean and on to his next adventure.

As he sailed on to his next client, he thought about Nigel and felt proud that he'd helped the village in Kenya. He believed Professor Wombatt would have approved, even though he had to use three wishes. He only regretted that he never got a chance to say goodbye to Nigel. He hoped one day he would find out how the boy had fared.

CHAPTER THREE

Leila Almeini and Cheemo The Hawk

THE ALMEINI FAMILY had left Syria for the safety of Canada after bombs started falling on their town. The Canadians were very welcoming, but Leila, eleven years old and the oldest child, missed the white stucco house they'd owned in Syria, with its flower garden, vegetable patch and Cypress tree.

When she'd arrived in Toronto a year before, she knew little English but had learned it so quickly that she'd become one of the best students in her fifth-grade class. She'd been lonely before Amal arrived from Morocco, several months before. Having a friend who also spoke Arabic made a big difference. Mrs. Sylvester, their teacher, had asked Leila to help Amal, who was finding English hard. They walked home from school together every day, holding hands and talking. It was January, and icy patches made the sidewalks slippery. Leila skidded on the pavement as she tried to keep up with Amal, who had long legs and was almost a head taller.

Leila wished she looked like Amal, who was tall and grace-ful. She had honey colored skin, almond eyes glowing over high cheekbones, and auburn hair braided into long thin strands and pulled back into a thick knot at the nape of her neck. Instead Leila was short and skinny, with pale skin and curly black hair that always seemed to tangle into a ball under the warm hats she needed for the wintry weather.

Their fifth grade class had other foreign students, but they were the only Arabic speakers. All the immigrant children were shy and careful when they spoke in class. In Syria no one dared question a teacher. Leila was amazed by how bold some of the Canadians were and said whatever came to mind. The boldest of them all was a boy named Billy Baxter. Mrs. Sylvester had to stop her lessons several times a day to scold him. Since there were two other boys in the class named Billy, she addressed him by his full name.

"Billy Baxter, will you please sit down!" she would say in a pained voice.

"I was only sharpening my pencil, Mrs. Sylvester."

"For a half hour?"

"Gimme a break!" he would say with a loud sigh as he took his seat.

Later: "Billy Baxter! Please do the work on the board and stop poking Annabelle in the ribs."

"Sorry! I was just trying to help her with the work. Gimme a break, Mrs. Sylvester."

And again later: "Billy Baxter! You're whistling! Do I have to ask you again to be quiet, or should I call your mother?"

"Aw gee, Mrs. Sylvester. I just love to whistle, and so does my mom." The whole class started laughing while Mrs. Sylvester rolled her eyes with exasperation.

She didn't want to admit it, but Leila admired Billy,

because he seemed to have an answer for everything. He was also very smart and got good grades, although he never seemed to be paying attention in class. She herself would have liked to be as brave as he was and say whatever she thought.

Even though Billy tested her patience, Mrs. Sylvester was soft-spoken and kind with the students. One morning before the lessons began, Mrs. Sylvester called Leila to her desk. "I have a surprise for you, since you've become such a good reader," she said.

She handed Leila a large illustrated book called *A Thousand and One Nights*. "Keep it as long as you like and then bring it back so other students can read it. I hope you enjoy these stories. They're very famous. If you can, read some of them to Amal. They can help her learn English faster."

Leila only had a few minutes to look at it before Mrs. Sylvester began the school day. When she turned the pages, she saw colorful drawings of men dressed in embroidered caftans with turbans on their heads, and veiled women covered with jewels from their foreheads to their ankles. Some of them were even dressed in clothes that showed their chests and bellies. Imagine going out in public with so much skin showing! She knew some Canadian women dressed like that in summer, but Leila found it shocking. She didn't think her mother would approve if she saw the book. She knew she'd have to hide it at home so her parents couldn't find it.

When Mrs. Sylvester started the math lesson at eight, Leila had to force herself to close it and concentrate on the problems on the board, while all she wanted to do was to gaze at the pictures and read the stories.

That afternoon, as she and Amal were walking home, the wind whipped at her legs, and snowflakes stung her cheeks. Leila hugged the precious treasure to her chest under the royal blue parka her mother had bought her in a thrift store, like most of her clothing. She was thinking about the colorful illustrations when Amal pointed to the sky above the park they were passing and asked in Arabic, "Do you see that beautiful bird? What's it called?"

Looking up, Leila spied a hawk circling the trees across the road. Its silvery wings were spread wide as the bird soared above their heads and dipped behind the tips of the trees. Then it seemed to fall out of the sky, head pointing down like an arrow, and reappeared with a rabbit in its beak. "That's a *hawk*," she said in English. "I used to watch them in Syria where people trained them to hunt, but I've never seen one as beautiful as that. Try to pronounce these words: *hawk, rabbit.*"

"Hawk," Amal repeated. "Wabbit." She had trouble pronouncing the letter "r." Mrs. Sylvester had tried to help, but when Amal spoke English she sounded as if she had a mouth full of marbles. Everyone in class had trouble understanding her.

"Good work," Leila said, as her teacher did when a student struggled with a lesson. "Mrs. Sylvester gave me a book of stories, and I'll read some of them to you on Saturday, if Mama lets me."

"I hope I can understand them," Amal replied. They had arrived in front of her apartment building. "I'll see you tomorrow."

"If you can't understand the English I'll translate them into Arabic as best I can. The pictures in the book are shocking but very beautiful. Wait till you see them!" She waved goodbye.

Leila continued home, climbing the stairs to the small, third floor apartment where the rooms were always too hot or too cold. She wouldn't be able to read the book until after dinner and hid it under her mattress. After school she had to care for her infant twin sisters, only nine months old, while Mama cooked. They always rushed to have dinner ready by five, because her father started work at six. In Syria, he'd been a civil engineer with a college diploma. In Canada the only job he could find was at a gas station, working the night shift, while he studied during the day at a local college to become a mining engineer. Papa was always tired, but he said one day they would have a better life.

While her mother cooked and Leila fed the twins, Tariq, her brother, watched cartoons on TV. He was only five and didn't have chores or homework, but he'd learned English very fast, even though he was only in kindergarten. "Why can't he help too," she asked Mama, who said that he was too young to care for the twins. Leila yearned to be free to read the book Mrs. Sylvester had given her.

That evening, after Tariq fell asleep in the small bedroom they shared, Leila turned on the light at her bedside. The first story in *A Thousand and One Nights* was about the adventures of a young man name Aladdin, with all the chapters that followed full of kings, queens, thieves, and spirits who possessed magic powers, called genies. The tales were so exciting she felt as if she was part of the stories and forgot that she was in her bedroom in Toronto. Even though she knew that magic didn't exist, she wished that she could meet a genie and ask him to make her a princess.

She read until her eyes blurred with sleep. It was the first thing she thought about when she woke up the next morning, but she had to rush to get ready for school and again hid it under her mattress, afraid that Tariq would ruin it or that her mother would take it away if she saw the illustrations.

After school she waited for Amal, but Mrs. Sylvester said that her friend was going to have an English lesson with a volunteer. Leila walked home alone, thinking about the story of Ali Baba and the thieves. Approaching the park, she looked up and saw the hawk, and it dipped low toward her as it spiraled above the trees. She met its gaze, and it felt as if an old friend had greeted her. Then it was gone. Even though she knew she was supposed to go right home after school, Leila crossed the street. She wanted to find the its nest.

It was a cold, windy day, with wind that whipped around her ankles. It had started to snow, and the frigid air burned her cheeks. She searched the treetops but wasn't able to spot the bird or its nest. Just as she turned to go home, she saw a blue bottle sail down in the wind from the branches of a tall Douglas fir tree before settling into a snowdrift at her feet. She took her hands out of her mittens to pick it up, and as she did so a genie popped out of the bottle.

The spirit spoke: "I am Gerald. I bear wishes to whoever picks up my bottle. I have just come from Kenya…."

"I read all about you, my magic friend," she said in Arabic. "What luck that I met you! How is Aladdin?"

"Who?"

"You know—Aladdin with his magic lamp. You were there, right?"

"Not me," said Gerald. "That must have been one of my colleagues."

"How about Sinbad the sailor?"

"Never heard of him. Now, I can give you no more than three wishes…."

"Yes, yes please! Here's what I want: please make my father king of a warm country, not cold like Canada; hot like it was in Syria in summer. My mother of course will be the queen and I a princess. We will live in a castle decorated with gold, silver and bronze. I'll be my father's favorite child and defend him. I'll be brave and able to defend myself when anyone picks on me."

"My goodness!" Gerald said. "That's about thirty wishes, but I can only grant you three."

"But Genie, I know you can use your magic powers to help me! I'm counting on you," she said, and kissed him on his fat cheek.

No one had ever done that before, and Gerald was so flattered and moved that he relented. "Well, I'll see what I can do for you. It will take me hours to arrange things, but as soon as I finish you'll see green smoke and hear thunder. Then the magic will begin." After he spoke he realized how hard it would be grant her what she wanted. What she'd asked for was nearly impossible, even if he could grant a hundred wishes. He began to wrack his brains for a plan that might work.

"Thank you, Gerald! I've always wanted to be a princess," she said, forgetting how cold she was, and how numb her toes felt. She jumped with excitement among the snow drifts before heading home.

She hid the blue bottle on a small bookcase near her bed, placing it on the top shelf behind a baseball hat that belonged to Tariq. She prayed he wouldn't spot it. At bedtime when he fell asleep, she began reading a tale about a captive princess who told a cruel king stories every night, so she would not be put to death. Each day the king waited to hear more and spared her life again.

Meanwhile Gerald's head swirled with confusion, as he tried to figure out which magic spells to use. When at last he pronounced his three incantations, he included so many details that there followed only a small puff of green smoke that was no stronger than the wisps from a match when lit, and thunder no louder than a toilet flushing. He knew his magic was weak because he'd asked for so much. He hoped that the little girl who'd kissed him would be happy.

Leila knew her wishes had come true when the walls of her bedroom began to disappear, and in their place she saw doors carved out of mahogany open to reveal a courtyard garden. The air was warm and perfumed with the scent of flowers. There, watering grape vines and flowers beds, was Mama. She wasn't dressed in the dark jacket and hijab that she wore in Toronto but flowing blue trousers and a silky yellow blouse. Her curly brown hair was tied behind her head with a golden scarf, and a pair of sapphire earrings sparkled in the sunlight as she moved. Bracelets of silver and bronze encircled her wrists, and bells around her ankles chimed softly with every step. Leila had never seen Mama look so beautiful and rushed to hug her.

She heard her father's voice from inside the palace. "Noor! Noor, my queen, where are you, *Habibi*?"

"In the courtyard with Leila. I'll be there in just a minute to serve lunch. Are you hungry?"

He came into the garden stroking his beard as he always did when thinking about food. "Of course. The King needs to eat." He laughed with that deep voice that Leila loved so much. Looking regal in a long white caftan and a turban with an octagonal ruby just above his forehead, he picked Leila up. As he did she smelled his familiar scent of tobacco and myrrh, and his beard scratched her chin. "My little princess, as lovely as her mother!" How proud she was of her handsome, strong father! She told him that she was born to be a warrior who would protect him, and he replied, "I need women warriors. *Inshallah!* May it be so!"

Inside the palace, they feasted for lunch on all the dishes she loved: the hot flat bread, the rice with nuts and raisins, and the goat stew, golden with spices. Tariq was very disrespect-ful; he sprawled on his tummy and burped, while Papa made excuses for him. "He's only five, Habibi. He'll learn," he told Mama, who scolded the boy.

It's not fair, Leila thought. *They would never permit me to behave like that*, but she said nothing.

After the meal the family curled up together for a nap. Tariq slept with his head on his mother shoulder, but Leila was at her father's side, holding his hand. *I will protect him*, she thought.

She was awoken by her father's cries. "Thief! Thief! Someone has stolen the ruby that gives me royal power from my turban. I took it off before we lay down, and now the magic gem is gone! Where is the palace guard?"

When he heard the king, the guard ran in from where he was stationed outside the palace. "Your Highness, I saw a small creature sneaking away from the gate. He was half-man, half animal, and walked on furry hind legs. I admit I was frightened, yet I chased him away. I didn't know he'd snuck into the palace or I would have captured the beast. Forgive me, Sire!" He fell to his knees and bowed his forehead to the ground.

"I could have your head cut off for not protecting the palace, but I'll spare you if you find the creature and recover my precious ruby, given to me by my father, and his father before him. The thief must have been the evil wizard, Osman, the shape changer. People say he often becomes a wolf and terrorizes the flocks of sheep and goats. Who else would dare come into the palace while we were resting? Only he would do such a wicked deed. Find him and bring him here for me to punish. Now go!"

"Yes, Your Highness." Calling for more soldiers, the guard jumped up and ran away in panic.

"I'll find the thief for you, Papa," Leila said. "I'll take my hawk, and he'll help me. I'm not afraid of Osman." Putting on the thick leather sleeve that protected her arm from the bird's sharp talons, she ran into the courtyard and whistled for Cheemo the hawk, famous for his hunting skills and magic powers. The bird was immortal and had served her family for centuries. Her grandfather had given Leila the hawk as a gift when she was five, and she'd hunted with him ever since. It nested in a tall cypress tree behind the palace and obeyed only her.

Cheemo's silver and white wings fluttered above her head before landing gently on her arm. "Find the thief who stole the king's ruby," she told him. His golden eyes flashing, Cheemo sailed over the palace toward the surrounding woods, and she dashed after him.

The hawk soon circled a tall oak tree. Looking up, Leila saw the thief sitting on a branch at the very top. "Give me my father's ruby, Osman," she shouted. "If you want mercy from the king, give it back now. If not, when I catch you I'll make sure you are punished, you evil devil!"

He laughed mockingly. "Ah, Princess Leila. You'll never catch me." Taunting her, he waved his claw-like hand to reveal the gem, glowing in the sunlight, and clasped between his thumb and forefinger. "You'll never lock me up—not Osman the most daring and clever wizard in the kingdom. The royal ruby is now mine, and I shall possess its magic powers, not your father!"

He was too high up and the tree too tall for Leila to climb. She knew the palace soldiers would come soon, but before then the thief would hear them and flee deeper into the forest in his guise as a wolf. She had to act fast before Osman could escape. Leila whistled and pointed. Cheemo rose from his perch and descended through the tree branches with lightning speed, plucking the ruby from Osman's fingers as the thief yelled in fury. Leila raised her gloved arm, and the hawk flew down and perched on her arm, while the stone glowed fiery red in its beak. The magical gem was inches from her cheek. As she reached with her free hand for the ruby....

"Leila, wake up! It's late. You need to dress and get ready for school." Papa was at her bedside, his hand stroking her cheek. He smelled of tobacco, coffee and gasoline, and he looked tired. "Hurry now. Mama is waiting with breakfast."

"But you were a king...."

"You must have been dreaming. I heard you say '*Cheemo*' in your sleep. Who's Cheemo?"

"Never mind." Leila stood up, the memory of the dream still so vivid she looked down at her hand, expecting to see the ruby there. She ached to hold it, so close had she been to possessing its powers.

She looked up to find the blue bottle, but it too was gone. "My bottle! Where's my blue bottle?" She ran into the kitchen where Mama was spooning yoghurt over fruit. "Mama, have you seen a blue bottle? I put it on the shelf last night, but I can't find it."

"Yes, I saw it, and I'm very angry that you left it where you did. Tariq climbed onto a chair and got hold of it this morning, while you were sleeping. He came racing out of the bedroom with that dirty bottle, laughing as if he were possessed by an evil spirit. I had to fight with him to take it away. He could have hurt himself if the glass broke. I expect you to be smarter than that. Now hurry up and eat breakfast. You'll be late for class!"

"But, Mama, where's my bottle?"

"I threw it down the trash chute. I can't have you bringing garbage home."

Leila ran down the third floor hallway. When she opened the hatch of the trash chute, the stink of rotting garbage filled her nostrils. There was no sign of Gerald. She hoped that wherever he was, he was safe. She had no time to worry about him and hurried back to eat and get dressed for school. In class she wondered what had happened to the bottle but didn't have any way to find out. She also worried that Tariq would find the book and ruin it.

Fortunately, Tariq had not found *A Thousand and One Nights* under the blanket on her bed, where it still was open to the page she'd been reading the night before. She continued to reread the book until she could recite every tale and picture all the illustrations in her head. Every time she read a tale, she recalled her dream and the ruby. Her dream melted into reality, and so did the stories. The kings, queens, princesses and beggars she read about became almost as real as people she knew. One of the princesses in the illustrations reminded her of Mrs. Sylvester, with her bright red hair and blue eyes, and a picture of a slave girl in another tale shared Amal's beautiful smile.

A month later she gave the beautiful book back to Mrs. Sylvester so other students could enjoy it. She hated to part with it and had reread the stories many times. She daydreamed about Cheemo and someday becoming a real princess, but she never saw the hawk again, although she looked for it everyday walking home from school.

Remembering Cheemo, she promised herself to help other immigrants like herself find success and happiness wherever they settled. That, she decided, would be her goal for the future as a woman warrior living her life in Canada.

Let us return to poor Gerald, who found no reward for his trouble, after he gave Leila her magic dream.

At seven o'clock in the morning he was still in the blue bottle on a high shelf in her bedroom. Leila and her brother were asleep nearby. Then the boy woke up and saw the bottle. Standing on a chair, he grabbed it off the shelf. As was required by the rules of Geniometry, Gerald had to offer this new client a wish, but Tariq didn't understand. He insisted that the bottle was a rocket ship belonging to someone named Sponge Bob SquarePants.

A woman appeared and chased the boy until she was able to grab the bottle out of his hands. She scolded him, and when he started crying she threw the bottle down a trash chute where it shattered into many pieces as it hit the bottom.

Wondering what to do next, Gerald lay in a pile of garbage. Before he could make a plan, a large vehicle with grinding gears backed up to the bin where he lay, and a mechanical claw lifted it up and dumped the contents onto a huge pile of other garbage. The truck carried its heavy load many miles, finally discharging it onto a mountain of spoiled food, broken glass, plastic containers and other refuse.

A genie without a bottle is a lost sprite, unable to find clients and out of a job. Gerald needed some magic, but he couldn't use his powers to help himself. That was against the rules of Geniometry. He was desperate to find another bottle. He drifted on a smelly breeze that blew over the garbage dump toward Lake Ontario. First, he saw a small bottle with a narrow neck that had once contained a medicine called syrup of ipecac. It was far too small for him. Then he spotted a plastic jug that once held bleach and was larger, but the plastic was opaque. He needed to see out, so that wouldn't do either.

At last he came to a glass bottle that was about the right size. It had a nice large opening in the top where once a cork had been. It also had a small hook handle and a narrow spout. The clear glass was engraved with the words *Hawley's Maple Vinegar, Product of Canada*. Gerald tried it on for size. He fit comfortably in the bottle's base, but it had a strong sour scent. He decided to use it until something better might come along.

He sent an urgent message to the college with his genie phone: "My blue bottle broke. Please have the Mighty Wind look for me in my new one with the name *Hawley's Maple Vinegar* engraved on it." Professor Aardvark replied that the wind was on its way, and he hoped Gerald liked his new home.

As he sailed away to another client, Gerald thought about Leila. He was sorry he'd never gotten the opportunity to tell her how they'd met. It hadn't been by chance alone.

When the Mighty Wind had first carried him to the park in Toronto, the blue bottle had landed in Cheemo's nest. The immortal hawk was living atop a Douglas fir in Toronto, after wandering the globe. Over the centuries it'd visited China, Venezuela, Finland, Ethiopia, and many other nations. Cheemo sensed where he would be needed next, and his mission was to help those in need.

Gerald watched as the big bird flew back to his nest and waited to push the bottle out until it spotted the girl in a blue parka standing below, gazing upward. As the wind rocked the boughs of the tree, the pine needles whispered "Inshallah." When she stood under his nest, the hawk shoved it with his beak and watched the bottle fall onto the snowbank, where Leila picked it up.

Cheemo had sensed her homesickness when he first spotted her walking home with Amal. The hawk knew the bottle contained a genie and hoped that Gerald could make her life in Toronto happier. After it saw Leila pick up the bottle, the mythical hawk soared away to bring hope and inspire those he helped to help other people in return.

CHAPTER FOUR

Champion Mouser

AFTER TORONTO, THE magic wind sailed for months in the clouds before setting Gerald down in a new location. When he landed, he stuck his head out of the bottle and saw nothing but stalks of grain wherever he looked. To the north were rows of wheat, to the south even more, and the same to the east and west. Where, he wondered, was he, and how could a client find his bottle in the middle of a wheat field?

The next morning Gerald heard a loud humming noise and realized a large machine was coming closer and closer. He cringed and prayed that the machine wouldn't crush the vinegar bottle. But no, just when he was sure he would be run over, the engine stopped. He heard footsteps crunching through the wheat, and a voice said in English, "Whatever is a bottle doing in the middle of my field, and how did it get here?" A large, dirty hand reached out and picked it up.

Gerald stuck his head out. "Hello. My name is Gerald, and I'm a genie here to grant you a wish."

A tall man was holding the vinegar bottle, and he smiled

to see Gerald. "Well, hello there, mate! What all are you doing here in Australia? How'd ya get here? I never thought that genies really did exist. I believed they were only in fairy stories me mum used to read to me."

"Well as you can see, I do indeed exist, and this is your lucky day! How can I serve you, my friend? I can get you whatever you wish? A new house? A trip to China? Money for a new car? Those of some of the things we genies can provide."

"Well thank you kindly. My name is Frank Appleby, and this is my farm that you see. I have acres of wheat that I'm harvesting and some rye, barley and soy as well. It's pretty quiet on the farm, but I still prefer living here by myself than going off to China, although it's a bit of a lonely life. I just built a new barn; you can see its roof from here. I really appreciate the offer, but there's nothing I need at present."

Gerald couldn't believe that he had just met someone who didn't want anything. "No gourmet meals, no new clothes, a fancy car, or a mansion? One client asked a genie for a yacht, and he got it!"

Frank Appleby laughed. "What would I want with a yacht in the middle of farmland here in Australia? I don't need gourmet meals. I eat simple food: the eggs from my chickens, the vegetables from the garden, and fruit from the orchard I have nearby. I can't think what else I might need, except perhaps… a cat! Yes, a cat would make me very happy."

"A cat?" asked Gerald. "Why can't you get a cat from a neighbor?"

"My neighbors are many miles away, and I don't know if they have cats and could give me one. But I need one badly; mice are eating away the grain in the granary, and rats have taken over the barn." He pointed to buildings in the distance, near a wooden house. "No matter how many mouse traps I set, I can't keep up with the vermin. Only a cat can rid me of the rats and mice, and that's all I ask. When I get through threshing the wheat today, I'd love to see a cat waiting for me."

Gerald had to admit that was a simple request and an easy job for his skills. He recited a short incantation and summoned forth a cat that would be good for killing mice and rats. Green smoke rose from the field and a thunderbolt flashed above his head.

"I think we're going to have a thunderstorm," the farmer said, as he looked up at the clouds. "I just heard thunder, so I'd better get going harvesting the wheat before it rots in the rain." He picked up the bottle with the genie in it, as he climbed onto the machine and turned on the thresher's engine. The air filled with exhaust as it continued through the field. It was a bumpy ride that Gerald didn't much enjoy.

At dusk he steered the threshing machine to the barn, and when Frank climbed down with the bottle, he found a cat sitting by the house waiting for them. It was a large, grey tabby with spiky fur and flat ears. Leaning over, Frank read aloud the words on the leather collar around its neck.

"**I'm called Champion Mouser,**" and "*Please treat me kindly*" were the inscriptions printed on a small tag that dangled beneath. Frank grinned with delight. "Welcome Champion Mouser, and thank you Gerald," he said.

As soon as the cat heard its name it ran off toward the nearby granary, and Frank didn't see him again for days. When he did catch sight of Champion Mouser, the cat was always running through the narrow stacks of grain in the silo, never stopping to be petted or fed. He saw the results of the cat's efforts right away. The granary, which had always rustled with the scurrying of little paws, gradually fell silent.

Frank understood that Champion Mouser was a serious

cat. He had a job, the mission that Gerald had given him. He was an executioner and didn't stop until every mouse and rat that he spotted in the granary and barn was gone.

The news of the cat's arrival spread through the colony of mice that lived in the grain silo. Those who met Champion Mouser suffered under his sharp claws and teeth. Most of them became so frightened that they fled with their entire clan to the fields to build nests among the remaining stalks and scrounge for seeds in Frank's garden. They peeked out of their new homes with care, because Champion Mouser knew where to find them and chased them through the fields if he saw them emerge.

The barn was a harder job. The rats there were big and strong, grown fat from munching on all the crops from Frank's garden and comfortable in their nests in the hayloft. They were determined to protect their territory. There was an epic battle between the rat king and Champion Mouser. The rat king squealed with pain, while the cat meowed and hissed as they wrestled on the barn floor. All the other rats watched in terror. Finally, the bloody rat king limped away with only three legs. Champion Mouser had bitten off the fourth. Trembling with fear, the rest of the rats abandoned the barn and sneaked away to build a new nest in Frank's cellar, where he didn't discover them until he'd finished harvesting his crops months later.

Gerald was very proud of the success of his sorcery and considered his job done. He was surprised when one day Frank picked up the bottle where it sat by his kitchen window and asked, "Excuse me, genie. May I please have another wish?"

"Another one?" asked Gerald. "I thought that I gave you just what you asked for. Why would you need another?" Knowing that he could only grant twenty wishes, he was trying not to give away too many to any client unless absolutely necessary.

"I want another cat because I'm lonely. Champion Mouser is doing a wonderful job ridding me of vermin, but he won't keep me company. I've invited him into the house, but he prefers to sleep in the barn, always with one eye open for more rats and mice. I would love a cat that lived mostly indoors, eats dinner with me, and sleeps on my bed at night."

Gerald thought about it. He understood that humans need company —preferably other people to share their days, whereas genies and elves are solitary creatures. He understood how far away Frank lived from other people and that he might be very lonely. It wouldn't be hard to conjure up another cat to share Frank's house, and so he agreed. Once more he spoke the magic words, followed by the flash of green smoke and a brief rumble of thunder. At Frank's feet there appeared a small white kitten with grey paws, sleek fur and dainty ears. When Frank picked it up, it started purring, and he kissed its nose.

"Thank you so much, Gerald," said Frank. "I'll name this little one Trixie, and she'll spend her days sitting in the sun, sharing my dinner, and keeping me company in the evening." Trixie became a wonderful pet, purring in his lap after dinner and sleeping by his feet at night.

The vinegar bottle sat, forgotten, by the kitchen window while Frank hurried to finish harvesting his crops. Gerald would've loved to be outdoors where the Mighty Wind could carry him to his next client, but he was stuck in the house in Australia until Frank might discover the bottle again.

In March, Frank finished the harvest and stored the grain for winter in the southern hemisphere. As the days grew colder, he had less work outdoors and spent more time in the house with Trixie. One day in April she disappeared.

Frank looked everywhere for her: in the cupboards, under the beds, and among the heavy quilts in his linen closet where she sometimes napped. She was nowhere to be found. He was heartbroken. Gerald heard him calling, "My little Trixie, where are you?" but she didn't appear. Nevertheless, Frank saw something was nibbling at the food he left out for her, and he didn't give up hope.

A week later while he was sitting in his recliner watching television, she appeared carrying a tiny kitten in her mouth, which she proudly laid at his feet. Then she went back to where she'd made a nest among Frank's boots in the back of the hall closet and carried forth three more kittens: in all two with white fur and grey paws, and two tabbies with spiky grey fur and flat ears.

Trixie was a wonderful mother to her babes. She licked them clean, taught them good manners, and scolded them when they jumped on the furniture or scratched the upholstery. Frank was overjoyed to have a household of cats for company. He gave all the kittens names, cuddled them until they squirmed, and spent hours watching them play hide and seek among the furniture in the den. Even though he was anxious to be off, Gerald also enjoyed watching them scurry around the kitchen.

When July arrived, and snow fell on the fields, Frank heard a meow at the kitchen door. When he opened it, Gerald saw Champion Mouser limp in, his fur matted and tipped with frost. The big cat went right to the fireplace where a log was burning and curled up in exhaustion. He'd worked long and hard, and now was his chance to rest and recover until vermin returned to the granary in the spring. By the fire he dreamed of dancing mice and scampering rats, and his tail twitched in anticipation of future battles. The kittens ran around him, while Trixie and Frank watched them play. After Champion Mouser woke up, he played with them too until the kittens bit his tail. Then he swatted them away with his big paws.

Come springtime in October, Frank discovered the vinegar bottle on the shelf, covered with dust. When he picked it up, Gerald asked, "Please put me outside. I've been waiting to leave since summer."

"Sorry, Gerald," Frank replied. "I'll do that. Your two wishes made me a happy man." He placed the bottle in his vegetable garden to wait for the Mighty Wind.

As the bottle lay among the carrot sprouts, the genie saw that the four kittens, now full-grown cats, were proving to be excellent mousers, well trained by their father.

The Mighty Wind came just as Frank was preparing to plant a new crop of wheat. Gerald said goodbye and set off for another continent and another nation, excited to meet a new client and face more challenges.

CHAPTER FIVE

Sylvie Arcoin

SYLVIE RAN DOWN the path toward the river with her fishing pole in hand. Behind her, from the doorway of her house, she heard her mother call after her, "Sylvie! *Arrete!* You know you have to do your homework before you can go outside! Come back right now!" Sylvie pretended not to hear. It was early April, and all the wild flowers were blooming in the meadows. She raced past the fields, into the woods behind her house, and hid from her mother by the river.

Once at the stream she baited her line and cast it into the water hoping to catch a trout for dinner. If she brought one home, maybe Maman would forgive her and forget about all the homework she hadn't completed. When she ignored their warnings about school, *Maman* and *Papa* shook their heads in despair and called her a wild child, *une petite fille sauvage.* They didn't know how to make her change, no matter how much they scolded her.

She loved to be outdoors at an age when most the girls in her class were more interested in pretty clothes and boys.

Sylvie still wanted to fish and climb trees in the countryside of Provence, France. She hated school. When her classmates teased her because she failed every test, she put her fingers in her ears so she wouldn't hear what they said. She had no good answer for Monsieur Dupuy, her teacher, when he asked why she hadn't done the homework. When he scolded her, she shrugged her shoulders and pretended she didn't care. In truth she did care but had no patience for schoolwork. When she got home after class she felt like she'd gotten out of prison and longed to be outside.

As Sylvie's fishing line floated in the stream, a strong breeze came up, rustling all the leaves in the trees and making small wavelets in the water. She watched as the current gently carried a bottle downstream toward where she sat. When the wind died down, the bottle drifted to the water's edge. Lifting it up, she saw a small creature pop its head and shoulders out of the spout. Sylvie, who was never afraid of anything, said "Bonjour" to the strange little figure wearing only a pointed cap and a belt around its waist, as if she had seen genies many times before.

It was Gerald, of course, and when he heard Sylvie he knew to speak French. "*Je suis votre djinn, Monsieur Gerald.* What's your name, and how can I help you?" He explained that he could grant her a wish, and even as many as two more, if needed.

"My name is Sylvie Arcoin. I want my parents and my teacher to leave me alone. I don't want to go to school or do homework, and they nag me every day about it!"

Even genies know that children have to attend school. "How old are you?" he asked.

"Fourteen. If I pass this year I'll have to go the lycée, and that will be even more work! I hate school. Besides, the other kids in my class call me stupid! Maybe I am stupid, but I don't care."

"I'm sorry, Sylvie, I can't make your parents let you skip school. You have to finish the year and then attend the *lycée*," which means high school in French.

"I don't want to go to the lycée. I'll be so bored!" Sylvie frowned and then smiled when an idea occurred to her. "Well, can you make me the smartest student in M. Dupuy's class?"

"I suppose so," said Gerald. He wasn't sure he knew a spell for that. "Are you positive that's what you want?"

"Yes! Then Jean Louis, who thinks he's smarter than anyone else, will no longer be the teacher's favorite. I will, and M. Dupuy won't get angry with me every day, the way he does now! Claude and Micheline who used to be my friends won't ignore me, because I'll be the best student in the room and not look stupid."

"Alright then," said Gerald. "I'll try, but I'm not sure I know how to do that." He waved his small arms and uttered a vague incantation for having more skill, like for a cook, but there was no green smoke or thunderclap. He'd never learned a magic spell for producing a good student, so he borrowed one for racing fast and changed the magic word "runner" to "student." That produced no flash of smoke or thunder either. *Perhaps I uttered the wrong words,* he thought. *I'll try another formula.* He remembered learning a spell for growing taller but changed the incantation to "becoming smarter." Still nothing happened. Hoping that something he'd recited would work anyway, he told her, "I did my best. Let's hope my spells worked to make you the smartest student in M. Dupuy's class." He retreated into the vinegar bottle before she could ask any questions.

Sylvie caught no fish, and when she went home for supper

her parents were still very angry. Maman said, "What will you do in the future? You have to get your "bac" and learn a profession. You can't stay a child forever." ("*Bac*" is a name for exams students need to pass in order to graduate from the *lycée*, or high school.)

Papa wagged his finger at her. "I'm warning you, my child, if you don't do better in school I won't let you come with us on vacation in August. You will have to stay here, with Tante Marianne." Sylvie hated Tante Marianne, their neighbor, a cranky old woman who made Sylvie walk her smelly one-eyed dog that nipped at Sylvie's heels.

"I don't have to study anymore," Sylvie said. "I'm going to be the smartest girl in the class. It's magic. You'll see!"

"What nonsense you talk," they said, shaking their heads in disgust, and sent her to her room without dinner.

The following morning in the classroom M. Dupuy called for the homework assignments. Everyone except Sylvie turned theirs in. "What, Sylvie? Once again! I will fail you if you continue like this, I promise. You'll have to repeat this class, even though all your friends will be at the lycée!"

"You can't do that," M. Dupuy, she replied, "because I'm the smartest student in this room."

All the students started to giggle, and the teacher told her scornfully. "How can you be the smartest student in the room if you never study? You have to read your schoolbooks and do the homework to learn."

Micheline stopped by her desk after school and said, "Sylvie, we've been friends since we were five, but I don't understand you any longer. Why are you so stubborn? How come you don't study? I know you're smart, and not lazy or stupid. Why don't you do the work?"

Sylvie felt very foolish. Even though the Gerald had said

she would be the smartest student, she realized that she would have to study to show everyone that she could learn too.

When she got home from school that afternoon she took out her assignments. For History she discovered that she'd missed a lot of the material that she should have learned since school began in September. She had to read the textbook from the beginning. That made the homework extra difficult, but she answered the assigned questions as best she could. Math was easier. She'd been paying attention when the teacher explained algebra and was able to solve all the problems. And so it went. It took her almost till midnight to finish, but she finally completed all the homework as best she could.

When she turned it in, M. Dupuy looked surprised but said nothing. When he returned the work the next day, she hadn't received very good grades, except on the algebra problems, which she had gotten all right. *I don't understand*, she thought. *The genie told me that I would be the smartest one, but I didn't get good marks on my work. Jean Louis still is getting the highest grades. I want to be the top student, as Gerald promised me. I'm going to go find that bottle and tell the genie his magic didn't work!*

When she went looking for the bottle, it wasn't on the riverbank where she'd left it. She cried for a few minutes and then became angry. *I will show them all how smart I am*, she promised. She went back home and started the day's assignments. The work seemed a little easier than it had been the day before, and as she started to study her grades improved day by day.

By June Sylvie was receiving excellent marks, but as hard as she tried she couldn't do as well as Jean Louis. Still, M. Dupuy had become much kinder, and her classmates no longer made fun of her. Her friends invited her to eat lunch with them, for the first time that year. She felt happier in school, and Maman and Papa stopped nagging her when they saw that she was studying.

During the final days of June, all the students had to take final exams. Sylvie studied for days. She was determined to do better than Jean Louis. On the morning M. Dupuy handed back the scores, she saw hers were the highest in the class. She danced around the classroom, waving her hands and chanting, "Now you all can see how smart I am! Didn't I tell you so?"

No one else seemed to share her joy. Jean Louis looked like he might cry, although he'd congratulated her politely. The sadder he became, the more she exclaimed, "You see. I really am the smartest student in this school! You laughed at me before, but not now."

M. Dupuy frowned and said, "Sylvie! Sit down and be quiet. I'm proud of you, but no one else feels like celebrating."

All her classmates wouldn't talk to her and acted as if she was invisible. Claude and Micheline avoided her at lunchtime, and Sylvie couldn't figure out why. Hadn't she showed them how smart she was? It was the start of summer vacation, and she felt very alone. She took her fishing rod and went down to the river.

Gerald's bottle had drifted with the current until it got lodged in some rocks downstream. The genie was waiting impatiently for the Mighty Wind to take him to his next assignment. He wasn't far away from Sylvie and could hear her talking to herself. *Hadn't she proven to the world that she was smarter than the other students? Why weren't the other kids happy for her, and why was she feeling so sad?* Listening to her, Gerald was confused. She'd gotten her wish to be first in her class. He didn't understand why Sylvie's classmates weren't proud of her, and why she was feeling sad.

She spent a lonely July, but in August she went with Maman and Papa to a campground on vacation. She didn't think much about M. Dupuy and his class, but when she returned home she was again lonesome.

She decided to phone Micheline and invite her for lunch the next day. When Micheline said she didn't want to come, Sylvie asked why.

"It's how you treated Jean Louis, that last day of school," Micheline said. "You weren't kind to him."

Sylvie remembered how sad the boy had looked. "What should I do?" she asked.

"Perhaps you should apologize to him," Micheline said. "You should learn to say you're sorry when you hurt someone's feelings."

Sylvie ran down to the river to cry. She couldn't deny she'd been thoughtless. Her conscience pricked at her, like an itch that won't go away.

As she walked along the bank of the river, she spotted the bottle among the rocks. She picked it up, and Gerald stuck his head out. He listened to her sob while she explained what had happened, how she'd boasted about her grades and embarrassed Jean Louis. "Do you think I need to apologize, Gerald?" she asked.

"Yes," he said. "Swallow your pride and say you're sorry. We all make mistakes. I can't help you with this. No magic spell can make this better."

"I understand," she said, "but how?" She carried the bottle with her to her bedroom and placed it on her desk while she thought out loud. "I can't phone Jean Louis since I don't know his number, and even if I can get it, what would I say if his mother answered? It would all be so embarrassing, not only to me but to Jean Louis as well."

"Why don't you write him a letter?" Gerald suggested.

"I think I can do that," she replied. "I know where he lives and can place it in his mailbox." She took out pen and paper and began: "Dear Jean Louis…," but then she decided that it wasn't a good idea to begin with the word *dear*.

Instead she wrote:

Jean Louis,

I apologize for the way I acted the last day of school. I'm very sorry for what I said. You are a much smarter student than me. I was just lucky on the final exams. I wish you good luck at the lycee. I hope to see you there soon.

Your classmate, Sylvie Arcoin

She ran down the street and put the envelope in Jean Louis' mailbox before she could regret it. It'd been hard to write that letter, but afterwards she felt happier and told Gerald about the letter. He said she'd done the right thing, and asked her to place the bottle by the river, so the Mighty Wind might find him. She placed it carefully among the reeds by the riverbank, as he'd requested.

Several days later Gerald was still waiting for the Mighty Wind when he saw Sylvie with Micheline. The girls came with a picnic lunch and swam in the river, just a short distance from where the bottle lay. He guessed from their happy voices that Micheline had forgiven Sylvie and was glad they were friends again.

By the end of the month the Mighty Wind had still not arrived. Gerald sent a text message to Professor Wombatt, who replied it would come as soon as possible. The Wind was overbooked, what with fetching and delivering all the genies around the globe, but Gerald was on schedule for an October pickup. Bored, he waited impatiently.

In early September, Sylvie went by bus to the lycée in a city twenty kilometers away that served all the students from surrounding towns. Her stomach jumped nervously when she saw the unfamiliar students and teachers, but after a few days she felt more comfortable. She liked her classes. They were more difficult than the lessons with M. DuPuy, but also more interesting. Maman and Papa didn't have to tell her to do her homework. Every day when she got home she spread out her books and worked until dinner.

Sometimes, when she went down to fish, she saw Gerald still waiting in his bottle and told him about how it felt to be in a new school. The lycée was big, and occasionally in the hallways she met her old friends, but she'd made new ones as well. She had to study much harder and didn't always get top grades, although she did well. When she felt discouraged she remembered that she'd only asked Gerald *to be best in M. Dupuy's class,* but not the top student in every school she might attend. She became content with doing the best she could. She was happy that Maman and Papa no longer scolded her. They still liked to call her "a wild child," but she knew they were pleased and proud at how she'd changed. When Papa came home from work and found her studying at the kitchen table, he smiled and tousled her hair. "*Bien fait, ma petite sauvage,*" he said.

She grew taller, and her old clothes no longer fit. When she saw the pretty dresses the girls in her classes were wearing, she asked Maman and Papa for new things *à la mode.* Papa pretended to be shocked that she no longer wanted to wear her old jeans every day. "Ooh la la! You now want to be more elegant than Marie Antoinette, Milady," he said, rolling his eyes. "What will become of you, my little fashionista *sauvage?*" She knew he was teasing, and when he finished having his fun he gave her money to pick out new clothes.

Sylvie spent most afternoons with her schoolbooks, and Saturdays at the cinema with her friends. The fishing pole sat unused by the side of the house, although she checked every week to see if the bottle was still in the river. When October came, she thanked Gerald and wished him goodbye.

When all the leaves had fallen off the maple trees surrounding the river, the Mighty Wind arrived and carried Gerald off to a new adventure. "It's about time!" he thought. He still wondered why, when he had cast the spells for Sylvie, there'd been no puff of smoke or thunderclap from the clouds over the river. He suspected it was because there was no such magic formula, so nothing had worked. He checked back with the professors at the school of Geniometry, and they told him none of his wishes for Sylvie had been successful. If so, he had three more than he thought to give to another client.

But then Gerald wondered how Sylvie had managed to pass all her tests and graduate first in her class. He wrote in his diary that he could never figure out how she'd managed, but was happy she had.

CHAPTER SIX

Akiko and Togo

THE WINDS CARRIED Gerald over cities, winding rivers, thick forests, and then above the vast Pacific Ocean. It set him down on a dirt road next to a village with tiny houses nestled close together. The homes were surrounded by small, neat lawns where children were playing together, except for one small boy seated by himself on a rock at the side of the road. When he saw Gerald's bottle land, he picked it up carefully and exclaimed with amazement to find a bottle with lettering in a foreign alphabet. He was learning *Hiragana*, the basic symbols for reading and writing Japanese, but had never seen the English alphabet before.

Gerald overheard and popped his head and shoulders out of the bottle to introduce himself. "My name is Gerald," he said in Japanese, "and I'm a Genie. I can grant you a wish, whatever your heart desires. But first tell me your name and how old you are."

"My name is Akiko; *Gerald-San*, and I'm five years old. I want a dog more than anything else. My friend Hiro has a dog. Can you see him?" He pointed to a boy playing catch nearby with an Akita, a beautiful breed the Japanese favor. The dog had a large head, powerful wide jaws, and was almost as tall as his owner. When Hiro tossed a Frisbee it ran, jumped gracefully into the air, and lunged to catch it. After bringing it back, the dog barked until the boy threw it again. Dog and boy were enjoying the game, and other children had gathered to watch the fun.

Akiko said, "I'll name my dog *Togo,* but it must be bigger and fiercer than Hiro's Akita. That way Hiro can't scare me any more by saying his dog will eat me in one bite. He makes fun of me and calls me a baby! When I asked my mother for a dog, she said no; the house was too small. But it's not. My parents and baby sister can all fit, so why not a dog"? He began to cry. "It's not fair! If Hiro has a dog and his house is the same size as mine, why can't I?"

"That seems reasonable," said Gerald. "Did your mother have any other reasons for not wanting a dog?" Akiko wouldn't look him in the eye, so Gerald knew that he wasn't telling him the whole story. "Be honest, or I can't help you."

Akiko scraped the toe of his sandal in the dust before admitting, "*Mama-san* said that it was expensive to feed a dog, and we didn't have enough money to care for one."

"I see!" His sad face made Gerald want to help. If that was the only problem, it would be easy to solve. "I can get you ten big bags of dog food," he said. "I'll have to use another wish but then your mother should be happy."

"Remember, my dog must be very big and fierce, so he'll protect me. He must obey only me and sleep with me at night."

"I will conjure up a dog that is bigger and stronger than that Akita, don't you worry! I learned how to do this in the College of Geniometry."

"Oh, thank you, Gerald-San," said Akiko, bowing. Gerald made a great show of waving his arms to entertain Akiko, while he shouted the incantations for the two wishes. When the boy saw the green smoke and heard the thunder, he clapped his hands with joy.

Gerald expected to see a dog appear, but instead from the house behind Akiko there came a sorrowful howling sound. It was so loud that the boys and girls playing nearby stopped their games to stare. "Aha!" he said. "Your dog is waiting for you at home. Go meet Togo." Akiko ran off, carrying the bottle with him.

When he got to the front door, a woman ran out with a baby in her arms. As soon as she saw Akiko she called out, "My son, don't go inside. I'm so frightened. There's a big, angry dog inside that appeared out of nowhere!"

"Don't be scared, Mama. That's my dog Togo, but I promise he won't hurt you." He ran toward his bedroom where an animal so large was crouching that there was scarcely space inside for Akiko. The dog was blocking the doorway.

When Togo saw the boy, the dog stopped howling and yelped with joy. It tried to climb out to Akiko, first trying to squeeze its head, and then its paws through the doorway, and when it finally wiggled out the other side the whole house shook on its foundations. Once in the living room, Togo jumped on top of Akiko, knocking him off his feet. He put his paws on the boy's chest and whined with love, his tone as gentle as the crooning of a mother as she cuddles a child.

"Togo, stop!" yelled Akiko. "Get off me." The dog rolled over and waited quietly for him to stand. He told Gerald, "I didn't realize how big Togo would be. But now that he's here, I want everyone to see him. " He beckoned to the dog. "Come outside, Togo. I want you to meet all my friends."

Togo began to squeeze out the front door as it had from the bedroom, and again the whole house shook. Akiko waited impatiently. As soon as they were outside, he told his mother not to be afraid and that the dog would obey him. But when Togo finally squeezed out of the house, it growled at her and all the people who had come to see what was happening. It snarled at everyone except Akiko. Then it spotted the Akita and ran barking down the street while the children fled in fear. Hiro's Akita scrambled beneath a picnic table to hide, the Frisbee still in its mouth, when it saw Togo, growling, race toward him with its teeth bared. "Gerald-San, please help me," Akiko said. "Why is my dog so angry?"

"Didn't you tell me that you wanted a ferocious dog, one that would scare the other dogs and command respect? That's what I ordered for you. However, if you call Togo, he will return. Remember, he will obey you, which is what you wanted. Call to him to come back."

"Come back, Togo," the boy called. Turning reluctantly, the dog ran back and then jumped up to rest its huge paws on his shoulder. As Akiko fell backwards onto the grass, the dog knelt over him and began to lick his face. "Ow! Your tongue feels like bristles, and your breath smells like fish. Stop kissing me, Togo, please."

All the neighbors had fled with fear into their homes. A policeman came by and angrily ordered Akiko to take the dog inside. Following his master, Togo struggled back inside through the narrow doorway. The house shook so badly that some roof tiles fell off into the garden.

Akiko heard his mother making dinner in the kitchen and went with Togo to see what she was cooking. He was hungry and told Mama-san that the food smelled delicious, and Togo seemed to think so too. It stretched out on the kitchen floor, wagging its tail with contentment. Accidentally, the dog's long tail knocked a pot of rice and bowl of meat off the table. Sighing with pleasure the dog gobbled up the dinner and licked the floor clean.

You can imagine how angry Akiko's mom was! She shouted, "Look what's happened now! Your dog ate our dinner, and now we have no food for ourselves. Take that creature back outside and leave it there!"

"Yes, Mom. I'm so sorry. Please don't be angry. Togo didn't mean any harm." As Togo struggled again to follow Akiko outside, the sliding panel door fell off its track and broke into pieces.

The policeman came running back. "Didn't I tell you to keep that dog inside?" he asked.

"Yes officer. You did, but my mom yelled at me and told me to take it out. I'm sorry. What am I going to do?" Akiko began to sob, and Togo licked away his tears. It then lay down in his mom's flowerbed, crushing all the delicate chrysanthemums and pansies. Akiko knew his mother would even be angrier when she saw what had happened to the garden she'd carefully planted. He tied the dog to a tree with a rope and went back inside, but Togo started to howl. It didn't want to let Akiko out of its sight and wailed all night with loneliness.

In the morning Akiko went to find the blue bottle where it had rolled under a chair in his bedroom. Gerald realized that Togo had become a problem and was hoping that no one would blame him. He wished he could get outdoors where the Mighty wind could find him and escape the mess he'd created.

When the boy found the bottle, he begged Gerald to grant him another wish. "Please Make Togo smaller, calmer and less ferocious. My mother cried all night, and my father is very angry with me. He says he's allergic to dogs and that I can't keep Togo. He sneezed all night."

"Did you know before I granted your wish that your father was allergic?"

Akiko didn't answer and wouldn't look Gerald in the eye. "Maybe he told me that a long time ago," he finally replied

"And when I asked you if there was any other reason that I shouldn't give you your wish, why didn't you tell me the truth then?"

"I wanted a dog so badly!"

Gerald had used up two wishes already, the first to create Togo, and the second for the bags of dog food lined up outside the house. It would take a third wish to make Togo smaller, and tamer, but then Akiko's father would still be allergic. Or, if he cured his dad's allergy – something he didn't think he could even do—that would leave Akiko with a large, fierce dog that was too big for the house. He realized the dilemma was caused by his poor judgment. He should've known that the boy was too young and couldn't be trusted. He, Gerald, should have asked more questions, instead of acting out of pity and pride. Now he saw only one solution.

"I can change Togo into a stuffed animal you can sleep with every night, one not made with real fur so your father won't be allergic to it. Togo the pillow will wait patiently and silently for you in your bed. You will learn to love him, I think. Will this be okay?"

Akiko sniffled and nodded. "Yes, but make sure he's a *small* stuffed dog, one that will fit in my arms when I sleep at night. Promise me that he'll never bite anyone, even my baby sister if she tries to hug him, or my mother when she folds my tatami in the morning."

"Yes, I'll do that," said Gerald. He whispered a new spell

which brought forth some green smoke and thunder. The huge dog was gone, leaving a pillow half as tall as Akiko. It resembled Togo alive and snarling, its large white canine teeth bared, as if it was ready to bite anyone who dared touch it. Although it wasn't cuddly, Akiko seemed happy. He picked up the stuffed animal and carried it to the kitchen to show his mother, who forgave him for all the trouble he'd caused. After his father fixed the front door and the roof, their home returned to normal. The family gave half the dog food Gerald had conjured to Hiro for the Akita, and the other half to an animal shelter.

Every night Akiko slept with Togo, and after a year the pillow developed holes and began to lose its stuffing. Akiko cried when his mother finally had to throw it away, but by the time he turned seven he no longer missed it. He hadn't forgotten about the strange bottle with the foreign lettering and a genie inside, but later on when he tried to tell his friends about Gerald, no one believed him.

Months later Akiko's mother found the vinegar bottle in his closet. She tossed it into the garbage bin before he could offer her a wish. One of the garbage collectors saw it and put it in the cabin of his truck to show the unfamiliar object to his wife. The wife became so frightened when she picked it up and Gerald started talking to her that she threw the bottle out of a window.

The genie had been in Japan for almost a year and was relieved when the Mighty Wind found him. Sailing away from Japan, he told himself, "I must be more careful. People aren't always honest with themselves, or me. Professor Aardvark was right. It's hard to know when a wish will produce unfortunate consequences. I have to remember the woman who wanted the purple house, and why it was unwise to grant her that wish without asking more questions. My visit to Japan was full of mistakes. I didn't use common sense and the result was that I had to use all three wishes. I'll have to do better in the future. Every remaining wish feels even more precious now."

CHAPTER SEVEN

Maxwell James Meriwether and Inez Abreu

THE VINEGAR BOTTLE lay on a paved sidewalk where the Mighty Wind had deposited it. Gerald peeked out the side and saw a quiet street. All around were lawns with perfect seas of green grass in front of the largest homes he'd ever seen. Each house had a private entrance fronted by an iron gate. On that very warm, early June day, there was nobody about except for a boy walking slowly toward him.

Suddenly a foot kicked the bottle hard. It went skidding over the pavement and spun in circles until it slowed, leaving Gerald dizzy and afraid that the glass had cracked. He was just getting over his shock when the foot kicked the bottle again with so much force that it flew in an arc and landed on one of the lawns. Angry as a hornet that's been swatted, Gerald popped his head out to see who had kicked his home twice.

A boy who was somewhere between child and teen stood

before him. "Why did you kick my bottle?" Gerald asked, in a voice trembling with fear and anger.

"Why not?" the boy asked. "Who are you, and what are you doing here?"

"I'm Gerald, a genie. I give people what they wish for, and I don't like being kicked around. You should be ashamed of yourself!"

"I'm sorry. I never thought there'd be something inside the bottle." He picked it up. "I only saw this old vinegar bottle, thought it was empty and had probably fallen out of a trash bin." He stared with curiosity at Gerald, who was still shaking. "Where did you come from?"

"My last client was in Japan. Where am I?"

"In Bucks County, of course. You must have heard about it! Everyone knows that this is the nicest area in Pennsylvania. My mother says this may be the most expensive neighborhood in all of the United States. This street has the nicest homes in our town, so that's why we live here."

The genie was feeling a bit calmer now that he saw the bottle hadn't even cracked. "My name is Gerald. What's your name, and how old are you?"

"I'm Maxwell James Meriwether the Third, and I'm thirteen." He pointed to a beautiful stone building in a cul-de-sac at the end of the block. "That's my school, the Pearson's Academy. My mother says it's the best private school for miles around, and she has to pay a lot of money for me to go there. Personally, I hate it. It's so boring! I don't like the teachers or the other students in my class. Look at me! This is the required uniform. I'm dressed like an old guy of forty who works in an office. I'd rather wear jeans and a T-shirt. like the kids in public school."

Gerald studied Maxwell's uniform. He had on neatly

ironed gray slacks, and a navy blazer was sticking out of his book bag. He was also wearing a long sleeved white shirt buttoned to the neck, with a navy blue tie under its collar. The tie was embroidered with a gold shield bearing the word *SAPIENTIA* written in red letters diagonally across it. The genie wondered what *Sapientia* meant. It was not a common word from any language he'd learned in Professor Mongoose's class. He agreed that Maxwell looked like somebody's father, and not a kid of thirteen, but he didn't say so.

"Maxwell, tell me what you'd like, and I'll try to grant you your wish."

"You mean you want me to wish for something magic, like on a star, or in some stupid fairy tale like *Snow White*? That's crazy! I'm not five years old baby anymore."

"But that's the idea. I've given other people of all ages wishes so far, and I'm approaching my limit. So, what would you like?"

"This is so mixed up! I don't believe in magic. Also, I don't have anything I want or need, even if you could do what you told me."

"Surely you can think of something. Do you play tennis? How about a tennis racket? Or Nike shoes, or another piece of sports equipment you've always wanted?"

"I have three tennis rackets. I used to take tennis lessons, but I didn't like them either. Tennis is too hard."

"An adventure? A trip to camp?"

"Naw. I go to sleep-away camp every summer for two months with the same boring boys who are in my class. The camp's in the Adirondack Mountains. We do the same things every summer: swim, sail, ride horses and hike. I used to like it when I was little, but not any longer. I'm so sick and tired of it all, and I don't need anything. My closet is full of clothes and shoes. Mom buys so much for me that she gives away almost all the stuff at the end of the season without me even wearing them once."

Gerald didn't know what to say. They were silent as the boy continued down the street, punched a code into one of the gates, and walked up the sidewalk to a large white Colonial home with an oak paneled door adorned with a massive brass knocker shaped like a ram's head.

Inside Gerald saw a large foyer with a black and white marble parquet flooring and a crystal chandelier suspended from the vaulted ceiling. The boy carried the bottle into a large living room carpeted in white with long beige couches standing like armies facing each other on opposite sides of a picture window. He collapsed on one of the couches, threw his book bag on the floor, and let the bottle roll across the room until it stopped by the leg of a grey marble coffee table.

The room was quiet except for the ticking and chiming of a Grandfather Clock against the wall. A few minutes passed before Gerald heard a door open and saw a woman wearing a uniform and apron enter carrying a vacuum cleaner. Immediately upon spotting Maxwell, she put the vacuum down and went to the couch. Pushing the hair off his forehead she said, "Maxi, you're so hot! I didn't hear you come in. How was school? How about a snack? I have some of those Oreo cookies you like."

"No thanks, Inez, I'm not hungry."

"Some lemonade or a glass of milk?"

"I'm okay. School was boring, as usual." He sighed. "I'll go change into shorts."

"*Bueno.* Then come down and do your homework, *M'hijo.*"

"The homework's so stupid!"

"Maybe for you, but when you explain me what you learn

I find it so interesting. I never got the chance to study all what you're learning in school. What the teachers teach you today, you teach me later, like always, no?"

"I guess so, Inez. I'll go change and then meet you in the kitchen." He left, and Inez began vacuuming, leaving neat parallel tracks in the wool carpeting, until she saw the bottle and picked it up.

Something about the boy and his apathy made Gerald tired, but remembering his responsibilities as a genie, he tried again, wondering if Inez would refuse him too.

Instead, when he spoke to her she gasped with delight. "A wish? I can have anything I want? Yes, I do want something very much! Seven years ago, I came to this country from Costa Rica, where I had a farm. It was so beautiful! I lived there with my husband and two boys, but when my husband died I had to sell it. I came here to find work to support my sons. I want to have my farm back. Wait, I'll show you!" Out of the apron's pocket she produced a cell phone and began to show Gerald photos.

Speaking in Spanish she said, "*Mira!* The house where we lived. My husband built it out of the lumber from trees in the forest around the property. You see our barn? We had there two cows, a mule and an old horse that was too lame to work anymore, but because Felipe and Gustavo loved him we couldn't sell him off. Of course we had a chicken coop, but there were foxes around and we had to keep it closed most of the time. Here's the river that ran behind the house, where my boys caught fish and swam." She pointed to a photo of a skinny boy. "That's Gustavo. He was only fifteen when I left, and I miss both my boys so much! Gerald, can you get my farm back? I heard that it's empty and deserted. No one lives there now. I could go home and be with my sons and my grandchildren. Yes! Gustavo married two years ago and has two little babies that I've never met. Felipe is studying to be a teacher and his wife Rosa is a nurse. " She showed Gerald a photo of a man and woman smiling proudly with two small children in their arms, and another of a couple dressed in wedding clothes.

As she continued describing the property her words were so powerful and the pictures so pretty that Gerald began to feel as if he'd been there himself. It reminded him of the farm on the prairie where he'd lived as an elf, and which he missed. He was quite sure that his magic could recreate her home for Inez. "Yes," he said. "I'm pretty sure I can grant your wish. You may need to fix up the property when you go back, but it will be yours. I'll make the magic happen somehow. When do you want to go home?"

She froze. "Wait. I'm sorry! I can't leave. What was I thinking?"

"Why not?"

"Maxi! Who will take care of him?"

"His parents of course. You're not his mother, are you?"

"No, but…Mrs. Meriwether, she's a very busy lady. Always meetings with friends, luncheons, committees, taking vacations. She's rarely home, and when she's here in the house, she's on the phone. Now she's in Florida visiting friends. Who'll take care of Maxi if I leave?"

"What about Mr. Meriwether?"

"I never met him. He and *la señora* are divorced. I hear he had two wives after Mrs. Meriwether, and some kids with another lady. He never sees Maxi, although once a month he calls. You understand now; I can't leave. Maxi needs me. But please give me a different wish." Wiping her eyes with the corner of the apron, Inez started to cry. "I want you to make Maxi happy. He's always so sad."

"*Cara Inez,* I'm sorry. I have no powers to make a person happy. I can get your farm back, but I can't change how people feel. As for you, it's not up to you to care for Maxwell. He has parents, and you have a family of your own. When does Mrs. Meriwether come back from Florida?"

"She told me in two weeks."

"Tell her then that you're planning to leave."

"But she'll be so upset! She tells me all the time how much she depends on me, and she pays me well. *La señora* is not a bad person!"

"I understand, but you have a life of your own. Tell her you'll be going back to Costa Rica in one month, at the end of June. She'll find someone else to hire as a housekeeper."

"But poor Maxi! He will miss me so."

"Perhaps he misses his mother more, Inez. I have an idea. What if I get you a plane ticket as well as the farm? I'll pay for the ticket, and you can fly to Costa Rica next month. Your farm will belong to you when you arrive, although I suspect that the farm animals you described have died or been sold. You can get others. Go home and be happy."

"Yes, I will do that. I see it's the right thing, even though I'll worry about my Maxi. Five years I've been here with him. But it's time for me to go, as you said. Fortunately, I've saved some money working for Mrs. Meriwether, and that will help restore the farm to what it was. But I couldn't do this without your help. *Muchas gracias!*" Inez reached for the genie's tiny shoulders as if she wanted to hug him, but Gerald was afraid that she might crush him. He popped back into the bottle, so only his head stuck out of the spout.

"You're welcome. Now please, put my bottle outside.

You're one of my last clients in my career as a genie. I want to go back to where I come from and retire. I also miss farm life and all my friends on the prairie, the elves and animals. I promise to grant you your wishes. Adios!" He settled himself inside the bottle and waved to her.

Inez lifted the bottle to her lips and kissed it. "Te quiero mucho," she whispered. He threw her back a kiss.

While waiting for the Mighty Wind, Gerald thought about those two wishes. He felt confident about helping Inez, but he also hoped that Maxwell James Meriwether the Third would someday discover that one special star he wanted to reach for—and then find the will to make it happen, because genies don't come twice.

Don't we all need to do that: fight for what we want most, when magic isn't there to help?

CHAPTER EIGHT

Calliope Kerrigan

WHEN GERALD LEFT Pennsylvania, he was aware he only had three more of the twenty wishes to give before he would lose his powers and go back home. It was likely this would be his last adventure. He would've loved to visit other exotic places, but he knew that the Mighty Wind drifted with no plan, depositing genies at random destinations. There would be many countries he would never see.

He sailed on the Mighty Wind over the vast Atlantic Ocean and landed in a patch of muddy grass separating a sidewalk from a road humming with traffic. It was pouring rain. There were few people about, but he heard loud shouting and cheering from a nearby restaurant. Peering out of the side of the bottle, he saw a sign that read "The Lion and the Lamb, established in 1833 by Thomas McCann, publican." The place had dirty windows smeared by raindrops through which Gerald spotted a giant television set on the wall broadcasting a soccer game. It was surrounded by cheering men with mugs in their hands. "It's a bar," Gerald thought. He recalled that the word *publican* was used in Great Britain to mean an owner of a *pub*, which Americans call a bar or tavern.

Just then the door opened and a man came out, cursing the rain, as he pulled the hood of his jacket over his head. Gerald understood that the man was speaking English as he waved goodbye to his friends. His pronunciation was so different from what Gerald knew that he couldn't understand the words.

The man burped loudly and stepped onto the sidewalk. It wasn't clear if he slipped on the wet pavement or tripped, but he landed on top of the bottle in the wet grass.

A group of men followed him out the door, laughing at the sight. "A pint too many, aye Paddy?" one asked. "Best get yourself home before you float away." They walked away shouting, "Yeah, Manchester!" while the man called Paddy groaned in pain.

"My bloody knee. Banged it on something!" Paddy reached down, pulled the bottle from under his leg, and read the label out loud, "*Maple Vinegar, Product of Canada.* How in the world did that get here?"

Gerald popped his head out, as he was required to do when anyone found his bottle. Paddy sat up and exclaimed, "Do I see a wee gremlin living in a bottle? Now I'm sure I must've had I had a few too many pints on top of the gin. This is very alarming. Perhaps I'm losing my mind, for I believe I'm seeing a goblin or some other unholy spirit."

"You're not dreaming, and I'm not a gremlin – whatever that is," Gerald said. "I'm a genie, name of Gerald, and I can grant you a wish." He hoped that the man wasn't going to ask for more alcohol, since it was very clear that Paddy had already had far too much.

"I'm just going to head home now, and by morning I'll

be in my right mind and not seeing ghosts. Good lord, I'm cold, drunk and soaked to the skin! Maybe a cuppa hot tea will sober me up."

As he struggled to his feet, Gerald said, "Well at least take me with you. I can't stay here in the grass with all this rain coming down." He also didn't like lying so close to the busy roadway, where his bottle might get crushed under a truck tire.

Muttering an answer, Paddy tucked the bottle into his pocket before lurching down the road onto a narrow lane. The neighborhood was so deserted that he passed only three people in the fifteen minutes it took to arrive at an old stone building. He climbed a flight of dimly lit stairs to a second story hallway that smelled of cabbage. As he knocked on a door, Gerald heard a girl's voice ask, "Is that you, Da?"

"For heaven's sake, Callie, open the bloody door. I'm soaked!"

When she opened it, Gerald saw a young girl with flaming red hair leaning on crutches. She exclaimed, "Da, didn't I tell you to take an umbrella? Just look at you, dripping all over the floor and stinking of gin."

"Perhaps I had a wee bit too much. It was an exciting match. Manchester United won! Callie, my dear, please get your poor old dad a cuppa tea. I fell in the wet grass, and I'm as cold as an iceberg."

"Okay, Da, but what do you have there in your jacket pocket?"

"It's just some bottle with a wee creature inside that was talking to me, as best I can recall."

"Are you daft?"

Paddy pulled the bottle from his pocket, and Gerald stuck his head out. "Hello, young lady. I'm a genie called Gerald, and I offered your father a wish. By the way, thank you sir for bringing me here out of the rain."

The girl gasped. "Well, at least you're not crazy, Da. I don't know how you found this bottle with Gerald in it, but you both deserve some tea."

In the kitchen, facing a cup of tea that the girl had brewed for him, Gerald explained about the three wishes he could grant Paddy. The man gently picked up the bottle and looked Gerald in the eye. "It's a kind thing you're offering me, but I don't think you can give me what I want. My daughter Calliope needs an operation to repair her legs. She was hit by a car several months ago and was in the hospital for weeks and had several surgeries. Gerald, can you heal the sick?"

"No, I can't."

"I didn't think so. Can you take away the pain she feels when she tries to walk? You can't imagine how much she suffers," Paddy said

"I understand, but no, I can't stop her from hurting. I wish I had that power, but I don't," Gerald replied.

"The doctors at the hospital in Belfast told me she needs more surgery right away, but there's no doctor skilled enough in Northern Ireland who can help her. The only surgeon who has the know-how to fix her legs is at the Excalibur Hospital in London, and we don't have the money to go there. Even if we did, that doctor, Sir Reginald Blanchard, might not take our case. I hear he's booked a year in advance, even for patients who are willing to pay thousands of Pounds above what the National Health Service provides. How could we afford him, even if he's available? Callie can't wait. If she doesn't get her surgery fast, her muscles will atrophy and she won't ever be able to walk again. She can't even attend school now. She'll be confined to a wheelchair forever without that operation. So thank you, Gerald, but even magic can't help us."

Paddy put down the bottle, placed his head on the table, and began to sob.

Callie patted his arm. "Come on, Da! None of that drama. It's just the gin talking. I'll be fine, don't you worry yourself."

Gerald thought about the problem and replied, "Maybe I can help. What if I pay for airline tickets to London? I can't promise the famous doctor will see you if you go, but you could try."

Paddy said, "That lot doesn't help poor folk like us Kerrigans. It would just be a useless trip. Besides, how can I leave my shop?"

"What do you do?"

"I'm a boot maker. I have a little workshop downtown, and many of my customers have been waiting months to pick up the handcrafted boots I've custom made for them."

Gerald said, "If it's your own business, you can close it up for a week or two. Just put up a sign saying 'Closed for family emergency. Will return soon.'"

"I suppose I could do that. Most of my clients have known me for years. They've heard Callie's story and will understand. Gerald, do you really believe your idea could work?"

"I'm not sure, but if you don't try, Callie may never get better. Don't give up hope. Let's plan a trip to London to find the doctor. I can pay for what we need." He remembered Professor Wombatt's warning about giving people more money than they could spend, so he budgeted the expenses carefully for the flight and taxis. He wanted to make sure that Paddy wouldn't spend any extra money on trips to the Lion and the Lamb, or other temptations.

Gerald bought plane tickets and a comfy wheelchair for

Callie, which Paddy had never been able to afford. Paddy packed some clothes for them in a duffel bag, and a week after he'd found the bottle on a patch of wet grass, they headed to London. He'd carefully rolled the vinegar bottle in his clothing so it wouldn't break and hidden it in the duffel. He was afraid that the people at the airport might seize it, if they discovered it. He needed Gerald, and knew it.

Everything went smoothly. The airport security personnel were very kind to Callie, and the flight was quick. Gerald, who hadn't flown in a plane since he was with Nigel in Kenya, found the ride very comfortable, as he lay snugly wrapped in Paddy's underwear. It was raining when the plane landed, and London was filled with people trying to find a cab.

In planning the trip, Gerald had forgotten that humans need food and lodging. He hadn't conjured up any money to cover those costs. It was five in the afternoon, too late to go see the doctor. Paddy and Callie were wet, hungry, and tired. Gerald had to use a second wish for more Pounds Sterling for food and a hotel. As they waited outside the airport in the taxi queue, he recited the magic words for the money they'd need. The thunder following his wish echoed among the clouds, while the green smoke blended into the foggy dusk.

When the extra cash fell in a bundle at Paddy's feet, he jumped with surprise and exclaimed, "Blimey! For a little genie, you can sure know how to make wishes come true. Thanks, Gerald! This will help us a lot."

After finding a quiet hotel where Callie and Paddy ate dinner and spent the night, they awoke to sunshine. After breakfast Paddy found a taxi, loaded in the wheelchair, Callie's crutches, and the duffel bag, before heading for the Excalibur Hospital, a large imposing limestone building. The mantel above the grand mahogany doorway sported a coat of arms with griffins holding up a banner inscribed in Latin.

At the information desk, when a guard saw Callie in her wheelchair he assumed they had an appointment and didn't ask questions about why they'd come. He gave them directions to Dr. Blanchard's clinic, Suite 457, and wished them a nice day.

Awed by the high ceilings and marble corridors that echoed with their footsteps, they went up in a large elevator and then down long hallways. "It feels like I'm in a cathedral, Da," Callie whispered.

"I know. I feel like a thief sneaking around Buckingham Palace," Paddy replied.

They came to a wide doorway, marked with the number 457. An inscription on the transom above the door read: **"Orthopedic Surgery, Sir Reginald Blanchard, Head of Department."**

Paddy opened the door and saw a sign that said, "Please have your National Health card ready for the receptionist." When he dipped into the duffel to get Callie's card, he also took out the vinegar bottle, placing it on the reception desk so Gerald could see the room. Without looking up from her computer, the receptionist took the card Paddy held out. She was about forty, slim, with brown hair and a pleasant face, although she looked tired. On her desk next to the vinegar bottle was a small sign that said, "Veronica Smiler, assistant to Sir Reginald Blanchard."

Miss Smiler was not smiling when she looked up and asked Paddy, "When did you make the appointment with Dr. Blanchard? I don't see the name Kerrigan on my list."

Paddy's voice shook with nervousness as he replied, "Miss Smiler, Callie doesn't have an appointment, but we've come here all the way from Ireland to consult Dr. Blanchard. My daughter had a serious accident and needs surgery."

She replied, "I'm sorry, but we have many patients scheduled today at the clinic, so you'll have to come back another time. I believe doctor has some appointments available next month, at the end of May. The scheduling office is on the first floor."

"Good lord, Miss! Don't you realize that we've come to London just for this? It cost us a fortune, and we've no bloody money left to come back in May. We used every drop of savings we had just to get here…." He was shouting, and she gave him a sharp look.

"I'm sorry, Mr. Kerrigan, but there's nothing we can do for you today. The doctor is a very busy man."

"You can't just ask us to leave after all this effort! For the love of God, Miss Smiler…."

Callie tried to interrupt, but the secretary said sternly, "Please stop shouting, sir. If you do not leave immediately, I'll call security."

Pounding his fists on the desk, Paddy began to yell.

Gerald decided it was his turn to persuade Miss Smiler. Intending to talk calmly and reasonably, he stuck his head out and began by saying, "At least let us talk to the doctor…."

When the receptionist spotted Gerald emerge from the bottle, she screamed and jumped back. Her chair rolled away from the desk on its castors and bumped into a file cabinet, dumping her onto the floor. The noise from the crash echoed off the high ceiling, as if a bomb had exploded. Afraid that they would to be thrown out of the office, Gerald ducked back into the bottle.

A door opened at the back of the waiting room, and a woman in a white uniform entered. "What's all this fuss?" she asked, as she spied the receptionist on the floor. "Veronica, what happened? Why are you crying?"

"I saw a creature like a hobgoblin in a bottle on my desk!"

"Where? I don't see anything." She looked around, but Paddy had quickly put the vinegar bottle back in his duffel bag. "Do let me help you up, Veronica."

"Daisy, you've got to believe me. There was some ghost, or little imp, in a bottle that spoke to me."

As she helped Veronica off the floor, Daisy said gently, in a tone that people use to calm upset children, "Now, now, Veronica. Perhaps you just had a moment of confusion. Everything seems to be normal. Just rest here for a moment. I'll take care of these patients." She turned to Callie and asked, "And who would you be, little miss? I don't remember seeing you here at the clinic."

"I'm Callie Kerrigan, and this is my dad. We've come from Ireland because Dr. Abbott at the hospital in Belfast said I need to have surgery to repair my legs right away, or I won't be able to walk again. Only Dr. Blanchard knows how to do such complicated surgery. We don't have an appointment, but I need to talk to Sir Reginald, please, if it's possible."

"Well, then, let me take you into the examining room, and I'll ask Dr. Blanchard if he can take a look at you. Come along then."

As she led them through the doorway, Paddy looked over at the chair where Miss Smiler sat, still sniffling and wiping her eyes. She gave him an angry look as they passed. "Sorry I lost my temper," he murmured.

As soon as Daisy left them alone in the exam room, Paddy took the vinegar bottle out of the duffel and set it on a metal tray. "Gerald, you fool," he said, "why did you have to pop out of the bottle and scare that lady? We're lucky she didn't have us thrown out on our bums."

"Why are you blaming me?" Gerald said. "How was I to know that she would get so frightened? Did you think it helped to pound on the desk and call her names? And what's a *hobgoblin?*"

"It's a little devil like you, who's always making trouble."

"After all I've done to help? You're an ungrateful loud-mouth, Paddy Kerrigan!"

"And who do think you are? You're just a stupid genie!"

"Stop it," Callie shouted. "Enough! You're both to blame, and arguing won't help. You two idiots have done enough damage. Now when the doctor comes in, I don't want you to say one word to him, do you hear me? These are my bloody legs, and I'll do all the talking. Is that clear?" Paddy nodded and Gerald ducked back into the bottle to hide. "Da, you promise?"

"Yes, Dearie." He hung his head in shame.

When Gerald heard the door open, he peeked out at the famous Dr. Blanchard. He was not at all what Gerald had expected. The man looked like Humpty-Dumpty, with a rotund belly and short thin legs. His head was round and almost completely bald; his face resembled a giant lollypop with blue eyes, a button nose, and a smiling mouth. He reminded Gerald of someone, but he couldn't figure who it might be.

Then he realized that Blanchard looked so much like his friend Alfie, the elf, that the two could have been brothers, if the doctor was as tiny as a buttercup and lived in the meadow. They shared the same waxy skin, round torso, friendly grins and round eyes. Gerald felt a pang of loneliness. He missed Alfie and the others and was happy he'd soon be going home. He'd enjoyed being a genie, but it was time to retire. Only one wish remained before the Mighty Wind would bring him home.

Sir Reginald had a deep voice, and when he spoke his voice filled the room and echoed off the walls. "Hello, hello, hello! I hear I have a surprise visitor from Belfast. And who might you be, my dear?"

"Good morning, doctor. My name is Callie, and this is my dad, Patrick Kerrigan." The doctor reached over and squeezed Paddy's hand so tightly that Paddy winced. "I've brought you a letter from Dr. Abbott, who treated me in Belfast after my accident." She handed him some papers, and he perched on an impossibly small stool to read them.

"So, Calliope Ann Kerrigan, you've come to find me about surgery. Is that right?"

"Yes, sir, and please call me Callie."

"How old are you, are where's your mother?"

"I'm fourteen. My mother is with the angels in heaven. She died five years ago, and it's been my dad and me ever since. We manage. He looks after me, and I look after him."

Dr. Blanchard laughed, and he looked so jolly that even Paddy laughed with him. "I think he might need your help more than you need his. Let's see if I can do anything to fix those poor legs of yours. Mr. Kerrigan, would you please leave the room so I can examine Calliope."

As Nurse Daisy led him away, Callie said, "Da, please be nice to everyone."

He leaned over and kissed her forehead. "I will, I promise."

No one had noticed the vinegar bottle on the metal tray, so while Dr. Blanchard examined Callie, Gerald was still in the exam room. He saw how gently the doctor flexed her legs and examined her wounds. Sometimes she gasped with pain but never complained.

The doctor called Paddy back into the room and told him, "Dr. Abbott was correct in his diagnosis. It's imperative that Calliope have surgery as soon as possible. I'll have my assistant get hold of her medical records, and then we'll schedule the operation for next week."

"Doctor, I know you charge thousands of Pounds for your surgery. I don't have the money for the operation, but I promise I'll do whatever I can to repay what we owe."

"Mr. Kerrigan, it's true there are extra expenses for the surgery beyond what the Health Service provides, but not thousands of pounds. For those who can't afford all the charges, I have a few benefactors who help patients in need, and Callie will be one of them. There'll be no charge for her care. But do you have a place to stay? We've a lot of tests to do before the operation, and then she'll have to remain here afterwards until she heals and can go home. You'll be here for weeks."

"Even if I have to sleep on the street and beg for food, I'll stay in London until my Callie is well enough to go back to Belfast!"

"Da, always with the theater! You should have been an actor," Callie said. "This isn't the London of Dickens."

Blanchard laughed. "I think we can find a better solution. I have an idea. Let me work on that. Please wait in the reception area until later." As he left the room, Paddy took the vinegar bottle off the tray and put it in his coat pocket.

They went back to the reception area. Miss Smiley was no longer at her desk. Instead a young man sat in her chair and greeted patients. They waited for hours until Dr. Blanchard was free. At last the doctor called Paddy and Callie into his office, which was very grand with walls filled with diplomas in Latin. Paddy pushed the wheelchair inside. As before, Gerald was listening in the duffel bag.

"Please sit down, Mr. Kerrigan," the doctor began, pointing to a large leather chair. "I've arranged for you to rent a room with my cousin, who works here at the clinic as my assistant. She is a dear, kind woman, but it took a lot of persuading to convince her to let you stay with her. She's finally agreed on one condition, something about a bottle she saw, but I don't quite understand the story." He opened the door to the office and called for Miss Smiler to come in. "This is my cousin Veronica Smiler. She said you frightened her."

"The Lord help me," said Paddy. "Me and my temper!"

Veronica Smiler sat down in another chair. "Mr. Kerrigan," she said, "I never again want to lay eyes on that bottle with the hobgoblin inside. My cousin, Sir Reginald, convinced me to do you a favor, but if you're to stay in my home, you must promise to throw away that *thing* first."

Gerald wondered what Paddy would reply, and what would happen to his bottle. "Miss Smiler, I promise you I'll get rid of it, word of honor," the man said.

Callie added, "Da, I think you ought to apologize to Miss Smiler for the way you shouted before."

"I'm terribly sorry for my bad temper and for frightening you. Please forgive me! Miss Smiler, I want no charity and insist on paying you for the room to let, but I'll have to mail you what I owe in installments. I promise to repay everything, even if it takes a while."

"Yes, I expect you will," she replied. "I'm not offering the room free."

Paddy nodded. "I understand."

"Now, my friends, I must see to my other patients," Blanchard said. "Callie, would you mind remaining in the clinic? We'll get you a bed in the orthopedic wing and get started right away on preparing you for surgery. Mr. Kerrigan,

Veronica will give you her address. She expects you there around seven this evening, after she finishes work."

"My darling lass, I'll see you tomorrow," Paddy said, as he kissed Callie goodbye.

"Now you be good, Da," she replied, and very softly whispered, "Gerald, if you're listening, make sure he behaves himself."

Gerald was listening, and he understood.

Paddy left the hospital whistling with joy, even though a light rain was falling, and his head was uncovered. He wandered around the city a bit before pausing in front of an establishment called *Knott's Pub and Grub*. "I think I deserve just a wee bit of gin to celebrate," he said, entering.

There weren't too many people drinking at that hour. Paddy found a table near the bar's counter and ordered a gin. Taking the vinegar bottle from his pocket, he said, "Gerald, my boy, I have to thank you. As you probably heard, I won't be able to see you after this evening. God speed to you."

Gerald stuck his head out of bottle and replied, "Yes, I heard. My work here is done. Just leave my bottle outside in a place where it won't get broken. I'll be fine. It's time for me to move on."

The genie looked around the pub. None of the patrons seemed to find it strange that an Irishman was sitting alone and talking to an old vinegar bottle. It was as curious to him as the people he'd seen throughout London, walking and talking on their cell phones.

He was unaccustomed to cities and didn't much like what he saw in London. Most of his former clients had not lived in tall buildings, like the apartments in Belfast and now London. He thought back to Nigel in Kenya, Sylvie in France and Akiko in Japan. They'd all been able to step out of their front doors and touch the earth. Toronto was the only city he'd visited up to now, and under a blanket of snow it had seemed peaceful compared to London, England. He missed the quiet of the countryside, with only the music of the crickets' chirping to color the silence.

Meanwhile Paddy was going on about how Dr. Blanchard would surely help Callie walk again. He told Gerald, "All will be well, just as I hoped. What a stroke of luck we had!" Whistling a tune, he downed the glass of gin and signaled for the bartender to bring another. After drinking it in one gulp, his mood darkened, and he stopped whistling. Frowning, he said, "You almost ruined the day with how you startled that woman, Veronica."

"Humph," Gerald replied angrily. He was still annoyed that Paddy blamed him for trying to help. "Are you going to take good care of Callie and be careful how you talk to Veronica?"

"Of course. But then my daughter is so smart she can take care of herself, don't you think?"

Gerald believed that it would be a huge responsibility to care for Callie after her surgery and during her recovery, and he said so. After watching Paddy down a third glass of gin, his eyes all glassy, the genie had an idea. "You know, Paddy Kerrigan, I want to do one more thing for Callie. So I'm going to make a third wish now."

"That's mighty kind of you, but you've already given us far too much money. I've got my pride, and no thank you! I'm a very good bootmaker. I charge a pretty penny for every pair I produce and can pay my own way." As Paddy spoke, he lifted the empty glass to his lips, hoping that a last drop might be there.

"Yes, you should pay for your lodging and food from now

on. I'll just make a wish for Callie's recovery." Gerald drew himself further out of the vinegar bottle, and waving his hands in the air, he started reciting a complicated magic spell longer than any of the others he'd ever used.

"What's that you're saying, mate?" Paddy asked, but Gerald didn't pause. When he finished, thunder echoed inside the pub so loudly that the walls rattled, and some framed photos of horses fell off the walls and shattered, scattering broken glass on the wooden floor. The lights in the bar flickered on and off, while sparks flew. The patrons shouted with alarm and ducked under their chairs. The room filled with green smoke, making everyone cough. "No cigars in the pub, please," yelled the bartender.

"Yikes!" Paddy said. "What just happened?"

"I uttered my last magic wish," Gerald replied. "It was the most powerful incantation I've ever produced, and one of the few that I ever recited indoors." He knew beforehand that the spell was capable of creating chaos. He'd been willing to risk it, because it was the only opportunity he would ever have to make things better for both Callie and Paddy.

Later, quite drunk, Paddy deposited the vinegar bottle at the edge of a park and went to find Veronica's house. Snug inside, Gerald waited for the Mighty Wind to find him. The pitter patter of rain tapped gently on the glass, as he thought about everything that had happened that day.

Gerald tried to chase away the suspicion that his twentieth wish might have been motivated by revenge. That would have been unworthy of the Genie honor code. True, he'd been very annoyed when Paddy accused him of nearly ruining the day, but concern for Callie led him to recite that final spell. Although Paddy had believed Gerald's last wish was more money for Callie, he was wrong. Gerald hadn't explained what he'd done, even though Paddy had asked.

He couldn't help laughing as he imagined what would happen when the man next ordered a glass of gin at the Lion and the Lamb, or any other pub. That final wish, the one that almost blew up Knott's Pub, was that whenever Paddy would try to drink gin or any other alcohol, it would taste as bitter as cough syrup.

The Mighty Wind came that very night for the bottle. It circled the globe three times on a farewell voyage before gently depositing Gerald in front of the old barn. It was a warm spring evening at dusk. He couldn't wait to see his old friends and the professors. Would Geniometry be the same as before? He'd soon know.

CHAPTER NINE

Home Again

THE OLD BARN looked even more dilapidated than Gerald remembered. Its wooden beams were rotting, and some of the supporting posts had started to buckle and looked as if they might collapse any minute. Propped open by some logs so it wouldn't fall down, the barn door hung on one hinge. Gerald wondered what would happen to the School of Geniometry if the barn were no more. Where would the genies and professors meet and hold classes?

Feeling very alone without the protection of its thick glass walls, he climbed out of the bottle. As he did, a face popped out of the barn. "Gerald! Welcome home." It was Professor Wombatt, and Gerald was delighted to see him.

"All your old friends are waiting to greet you inside," the professor said. "Some of the genies who graduated with you have returned; others are still traveling the globe to bestow their twenty wishes. Did you know that we professors keep track of where all our graduates go, and how they succeed?" Gerald shook his head. "We admired how clever you were.

Of course you made some mistakes, but we all did. You've done an outstanding job and deserve a rest after all that effort. Come inside and say hello. We all want to say how much we appreciate your work."

As Gerald walked in the door, he saw yellow balloons decorated with the words "Welcome home" tied to the old wagon, which tilted dangerously to one side. The metal axle had rusted and was almost split in half. He was immediately surrounded by friendly faces, all wanting to hear about his travels. Professors Aardvark and Mongoose greeted him warmly. He recognized his old friends Alfie, Suzette, other elves, and former genies. They all exchanged stories about their adventures. Everybody welcomed him, and the party in his honor made him happy to be home.

Professor Aardvark told Gerald, "We have a special surprise for all the genies who return. Come see our new device." In the corner of the barn sat a shiny machine with a camera and a screen, similar to computers Gerald had seen in London. "This is our GenieCam. With this all the returning genies can see how their clients are faring and can ask them about their lives. You'll view them on the screen, and they'll see you as a virtual camera projection. Would you like to find out how all your clients are presently?"

"Of course! I've been wondering about them all. I have no idea of the time I spent traveling the earth."

"We keep careful statistics on all our genies. You were gone twenty-five years, three months, and two days in people time from the moment you first left, and you had nine clients. Using the map of the world on the screen, point to any country that you visited, and the machine will find your client. Don't be surprised how they've all changed," the professor added. "Many are much older now than when you met them.

Let's get started. I think your first client was in Chile. Point to that country and click on the mouse to find him."

Gerald pointed the cursor on the map to Chile. On the screen he saw a man on a motorcycle weaving in and out of heavy traffic in Santiago, the capital city. The boy, Julio Vargas, who'd been seven when he'd asked for a bicycle many years before, was now a grown man. He waved to Gerald, but the roar of his motorcycle prevented them from talking. "I hope he stays alive among all those cars," Gerald said. "I wonder what happened to the bicycle I gave him, but it's too dangerous to ask him now. The bicycle was a lot safer than a motorcycle."

"Of course. Didn't you give someone else a motorcycle?" the professor asked Gerald. "Wasn't it for a man in Kenya."

"Yes," Gerald admitted, "but I couldn't give that man Peter any gasoline, of course. He wasn't my client, but the motorcycle allowed my client Nigel to get back to his village."

"Would you like to see how Nigel's doing today?"

"I would. He was such a brave kid," Gerald replied. He pointed to Kenya and found Nigel, now a tall man dressed in an impressive navy uniform with gold buttons and braided tassels. He was standing in front of an enormous airplane and smiling proudly, like a father showing off his baby. As Gerald moved the controls of the GenieCam, the picture became clearer and zoomed in on Nigel's face.

Smiling with pride, Nigel said, "Hello there, Gerald, my friend. I'm thirty-four now, no longer the starving boy you met. I'm now Captain Consobolo, a pilot for Global Access Airlines, with my home base here in Nairobi. I'm about to take the controls of this plane and head to Cairo, Egypt. I love my profession and have you to thank for it. You inspired me to study hard and I did, winning a scholarship to go university in England, and then to flight school. I fly to big cities: Paris,

Tokyo, Buenos Aires, and New York, and have visited many countries. You were my mentor. Thank you for everything you did." He took off his hat and waved goodbye before heading toward the cockpit of the plane. Gerald waved back.

"He was my third client," he told the professor. "My second one was a woman in Spain, named Norma Caceres, who wanted to have children. I was new at being a genie and did something foolish. In my enthusiasm I gave her triplets. I wonder how she and her husband fared." He found Barcelona, Spain and clicked to see an elderly man and women in a parlor surrounded by many people, from tiny children to adults. "*Buenos Dias*," Gerald said. "Do you remember me, your Genie Gerald?"

"Indeed I do," said the woman at the center of the group." The room was so loud with voices that Gerald could barely hear her. "I'm Norma, the woman who bore triplets. I'm now sixty years old, with more gray hair every day. You can see our entire family. My two daughters and one son all have married, and my husband Juan and I have twelve grandchildren! It wasn't easy raising such a big brood, but now we're older we feel fortunate that we have so many wonderful grandbabies, an entire new generation. Thank you, Gerald! We're lucky to have met you." Her husband waved to Gerald as a small child scrambled to sit on his lap.

"Goodbye and good wishes to you all," Gerald replied.

"I believe your fourth client was a girl named Leila in Toronto, Canada," said Aardvark. When Gerald pointed the curser on Canada, it focused on Ottawa, the capital city, not Toronto where Leila once had lived.

Gerald recognized Leila immediately although she was now a grown woman. She still had curly black hair in a cloud around her face and the big smile he remembered from the park in Toronto. She saw him and said, "I've never forgotten you and the dream you gave me, Gerald. I'm living now with my husband and family in Ottawa. I've become an attorney to help new immigrants and advance women's rights. I don't know what happened to my friend Amal, but I do know about another classmate in Mrs. Sylvester's fifth grade classroom. His name was Billy Baxter. Look at this!"

She laughed and held out a newspaper with a headline that read,

WILLIAM H. (BILL) BAXTER ELECTED TO HOUSE OF COMMONS FROM TORONTO.

"He was the class clown in fifth grade. All the kids called him *Silly Billy*, but now look what he's achieved! He always knew what he wanted and how to get attention. It's no surprise you got your break, Billy Baxter!" she said, laughing. "Thank you for your three wishes, Gerald. Maybe someday you'll come visit me and my family here in Ottawa."

"Thanks for inviting me," he replied. "Keep up the good work you're doing."

Next Gerald looked for Australia on the GenieCam. The camera took a minute to locate Frank Appleby's farm in that big country. Then it focused on the grassy yard behind Frank's little house. It was just as Gerald remembered it, with the barn and tall grain silo nearby. A tractor emerged from the barn with the farmer at the wheel. He turned up the throttle, and as it chugged past Gerald recalled how noisy the old machine was. Frank waved to Gerald but drove off without stopping to say hello.

The genie zoomed in on the silo. At its base sat three cats; two were seated guarding the tower and another circled it, searching for mice. He scanned the yard and spotted a cat in the trees, cats among the flower beds, and others playing on the grass. Kittens were mewing in the barn, while a mother cat raced toward it.

Finally he turned the camera lens toward the kitchen steps, where two cats were cuddling. The smaller one with white fur and gray paws lay purring with her eyes closed, while behind her the larger cat with grey fur licked her ears. Gerald spotted a tag attached to its collar but couldn't read it. He wasn't sure but wanted to believe they were the once ferocious Champion Mouser and Trixie, Frank's first cats. By this time they would be the great-great-great grandparents of all the other cats. The two wishes Gerald granted Frank appeared to have produced an army. He felt proud of how well his wishes had worked to help Frank farm his land without being infested with vermin.

Next, he searched for Sylvie in France and found a tall, slim woman standing in a forest of beech trees. "*Bonjour*, Sylvie," he said. "Do you remember me?"

"No," she said. "Who are you?"

"I'm Gerald, the genie. You were one of my clients when you were younger. I tried to help you become a better student when you were in Monsieur Dupuy's class. I don't think I succeeded in producing any magic for you, but I did my best."

"This is very strange. I don't remember you at all, but I can't recall much from that year when I was in Monsieur Dupuy's class. I know that at some point in spring of that year I finally decided to apply myself to my studies. I hated school before then and was lazy. I did well on the final exams and went on to study for my bac. After finishing the lycée, I decided to become a park ranger. I studied Forestry and Ecology at a university in southern France and am now stationed here in the province of Lorraine. I live in barracks at a campsite. My colleagues and I maintain the woods to prevent over settlement and protect the animals' habitat. I love my work! It's perfect for me, since I've always enjoyed being outdoors." She heard a noise somewhere in the woods and turned to look behind her. "I heard there's a wildcat prowling in the forest, and I have to go find it. *Au revoir.*" She waved goodbye and headed into the distance among the trees.

Gerald then focused the camera on Japan, where years before he'd met a very young boy named Akiko and had given him a ferocious dog. It had been one of the few adventures where he'd failed to use common sense, but it had taught him to use his magic more carefully.

The camera found Akiko in a park in the city of Kyoto. As years before, Akiko greeted Gerald formally, addressing him as "Gerald-San" and bowing. He said he was seventeen and studying at a university in Kyoto where he lived with other students. They chatted for a minute, and then Akiko said, "Gerald-San, I have something to show you. Look!" He pointed to the grass. When Gerald focused the GenieCam toward Akiko's feet, he saw a miniature poodle on a leash. The boy picked up the dog, and when it saw Gerald's image on the camera, it barked furiously. "I named him Togo," Akiko said, grinning. "He's ferocious like the dog you gave me, but only for a minute. When he calms down, he'll jump on your lap and lick your face." Gerald wished Akiko good luck with the puppy and left Japan.

He looked for Inez in Costa Rica and found her planting tomatoes in a garden behind her farmhouse. Several grandchildren were running around the grass nearby, and when they spotted Gerald on the GenieCam, they screamed in fear. Inez comforted them, saying that Gerald was an old friend. He saw that his visit was upsetting them and said that he'd better sign off. She replied, "You can see I'm very happy here. Thanks for all you've done! Please go visit Maxi. He misses me. Perhaps you can cheer him up."

"I'll try," Gerald said and sent her his best for the future. Pointing the GenieCam toward the United States, he found Maxwell James Meriwether in the big mansion in Pennsylvania. The boy was seated in his bedroom at a desk, writing a letter. "Hello, Maxwell," Gerald said. "Do you remember me?"

"I sure do! Can I have the three wishes you owe me now?"

"I'm sorry. I used up all my powers and am no longer officially a genie, just a retired elf."

Sighing with frustration, Maxwell put his head on the desk. "Oh no! That's too bad, because all I want is to go visit Inez. It's been two years since she left, and nothing's the same. My mother hired another housekeeper named Ana. She's nice, but she's not my friend, like Inez was. I talk on my cell phone to Inez all the time, and she sends me photos of her farm. It's so green and beautiful! She's very happy to be back with her sons and grandchildren. Mom says I can go visit her as soon as I'm sixteen, but I hate waiting! My sixteenth birthday is in May, so next summer I'll fly to Costa Rica. If you could grant me a wish, I'd have you send me there today."

Gerald replied, "You'll have a wonderful time next summer in Costa Rica with Inez, and when you come back you can finish high school, and then go to college. After that you'll be old enough to a plan your own life. Choose wisely! Costa Rica is beautiful. Good luck, and enjoy your trip."

Last Gerald remembered Callie Kerrigan. He'd been worrying about her and hoping the surgery on her knees had helped. He also wanted to know how Paddy had fared in London after he left, and if he'd taken good care of her while she recuperated.

When he focused the camera on Belfast, he found Callie

walking with a cane on a sidewalk damp with rain. Under a winter jacket she wore a green plaid school uniform and carried a backpack. "Gerald!" she exclaimed. "It's so nice to see you again. Look at me! I'm walking without crutches, although I still have a way to go before I can throw away this bloody cane." She laughed, and Gerald remembered with affection how cheerful she'd always been. "I went back to school in September, and I intend to get a first when I do exams in June. Over Christmas holiday Da and I are flying back to London. Sir Reginald has to perform more surgery on the legs, now that I'm stronger."

"And how's our Paddy doing?"

Laughing again, as her red curls danced on her shoulders, she replied, "He's making a pair of boots as a gift for Sir Reginald. Oh, and by the way he no longer drinks gin. Can you imagine that? He just stopped and won't tell me why, but of course I'm very happy that he no longer comes home pickled like before. One more thing—we'll be staying with Veronica Smiler next month when we go to London. Do you remember her?"

"I do," Gerald said.

"Da and Veronica became great friends when he stayed with her last year. He calls her all the time. I think he's sweet on her, to tell the truth. Can you imagine?"

"No, I can't," Gerald replied, "but I'm happy he's sober now. It's great to see you on your feet and doing better! Good luck in London, and give Paddy my best."

"Thanks you so much for everything, my little hobgoblin."

Gerald blew her a kiss. He would never forget her pluck and courage. Although Paddy had been his client, all his final three wishes were on her behalf, and he was proud that he'd helped her.

Professor Aardvark turned off the GenieCam. "Gerald," he said, "I'm sad to tell you that now you've seen how all your clients are faring, you have to say goodbye to them. They all seem to be doing well. You won't be able to contact them again. Like parents whose children are grown, you have to let them go. Genies are only permitted one opportunity to use the GenieCam. Treasure those memories. It's time for you to relax, join us for parties, make new friends, and help the few elves who aspire to become genies."

"Thank you, Professor, for giving me the opportunity to travel around the globe and meet these people. I've had wonderful adventures! Still, seeing my clients for the last time makes me feel sad, as if they were my children, as you said."

"We need you here. I'm not sure how long the College of Geniometry will continue to exist. There aren't too many elves left here, and every class I teach is smaller than the one before. I want you to teach new recruits if we have any."

Gerald didn't want to believe that the college might no longer exist in the future. He prayed more elves would want to become genies, as before.

He thanked Professor Aardvark for his offer and went to say goodbye to his faithful companion, the vinegar bottle. Dirty, with a crack in its base and a chip on the spout, it lay almost hidden among the tall grasses. He was grateful it had seen him safely home. Although it wasn't as beautiful as the blue one, it had protected him for many years. "Goodbye, old friend," he said.

When he looked around at the fields where he'd lived as an elf, he spied a pair of robins chattering noisily as the mother brooded over a set of eggs. Those eggs probably held the grandchildren or even great-great grandchildren of the robins he had once known in the same nest of the old tree.

He hoped he could make friends with the hatchlings and all the new generations of the animals he'd once known. That would be all he could do in the future: make new friends, treasure the old ones, and help guide a new class in the science of Geniometry, if there would be one. He settled down near the pond and began writing his memoir, which I have copied here for all to read.

✑

When I returned to that field in Kansas ten years later, the oak tree where I'd met Gerald was gone. The old barn and corn fields had disappeared as well. Instead a housing development had been built where the fields once stood. It held shiny new homes bordered by neat, white sidewalks on streets with names like *Elm, Maple,* and *Oak.* I thought those names were strange because I saw no actual trees on those streets, just telephone poles. It made me sad to think that progress takes away many places we once treasured, even as it gives us new comforts.

I was happy to find Gerald's diary, its pages yellow with age and stained with water spots, lying nearby among the overgrown grass. A little further away, I spotted the little pond with frogs still sleeping on the lily pads under the maple trees, and I heard robins chirping above in their branches. The scene made me wonder if those creatures missed Gerald and the other elves who used to live there, as I did.

I took the diary home, and this book is my effort to transcribe what he wrote about all his adventures. I don't want him or his good deeds to be forgotten.

I hope the School of Geniometry still exists somewhere. Don't we all need some magic in our lives?

THE END

Lucy Lehman is a retired teacher of ESL and foreign language presently living in San Diego.

After graduating from Wellesley College, she worked for a year in Rome and then studied at the Sorbonne the following year. She holds a MA in French from Columbia University.

THE ADVENTURES OF GERALD THE GENIE is her first published novel and was inspired by three of her granddaughters. She spends as much time as possible with her children and their children, who range in age from twenty to two years old.

She is presently working on a Romantic Comedy and hopes to publish that soon.

www.ingramcontent.com/pod-product-compliance
Lightning Source LLC
Chambersburg PA
CBHW051814050726
47598CB00006B/2553